MURDER

on the

Orford Mountain Railway

NICK FONDA

MURDER
on the
Orford Mountain Railway

Baraka
Books

Montréal

ISBN 978-1-77186-246-2 pbk; 978-1-77186-247-9 epub; 978-1-77186-248-6 pdf

Cover illustration by Beatrice Multhaupt
Illustrations on pages 4, 8 and 134 by Gaby Béland
Book design and cover by Folio infographie
Editing by Robin Philpot
Proofreading by Blossom Thom

Legal Deposit, 2nd quarter 2021
Bibliothèque et Archives nationales du Québec
Library and Archives Canada
Published by Baraka Books of Montreal
Printed and bound in Quebec

Trade Distribution & Returns
Canada – UTP Distribution: UTPdistribution.com

United States
Independent Publishers Group: IPGbook.com

We acknowledge the support from the Société de développement des entreprises culturelles (SODEC) and the Government of Quebec tax credit for book publishing administered by SODEC.

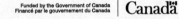

Part 1

THE ORFORD MOUNTAIN RAILWAY

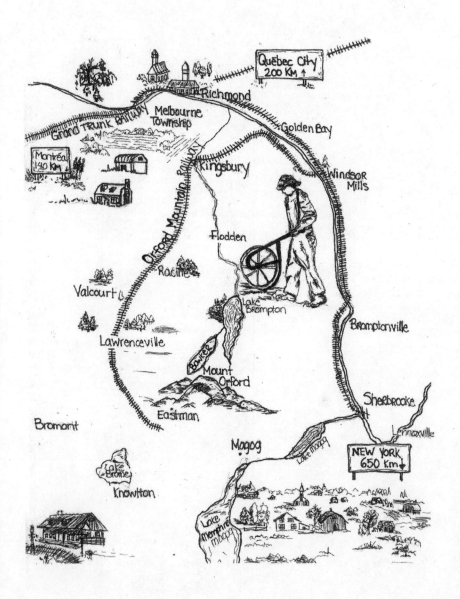

Chapter 1

Thank you, Margaret, for that very kind introduction, and good afternoon to everyone. I'm pleased and flattered that so many of you are here for this presentation on the Melbourne Murder, as it was called back in 1905, although it could be referred to, just as correctly, as the murder on the Orford Mountain Railway. The specific site of the crime was on a stretch of rail line that was under construction in Melbourne Township at the time.

A few months ago, when it was suggested I give this talk, I didn't expect I'd be giving it here in the church hall, or that the hall would be this full!

Welcome to all of you, and thank you for coming.

To start at the beginning, it was at the end of the summer, just after our summer students had left, when I realized what I had found, by accident really. The next day I called Margaret and told her, and two weeks after that, I presented what I'd found at the monthly board meeting. Brenda, who is the Historical Society's activities co-ordinator, thought that it was a story that should be shared with the membership at large. Hence, this afternoon's Tea & Talk on the Melbourne Murder, a tragic event that happened well over a century ago.

Today's presentation is essentially the same one that I gave at the board meeting. The only difference is that while it was feasible to pass around the diary and the newspaper articles to the half-dozen board members sitting at the table, it's difficult to do the same thing with a crowd this size. However, you won't miss a thing because—thanks to Benoît—all the relevant documents have been digitized and you'll be able to see them here on the screen.

I have to thank Benoît for all his help with the photography. We spent three days getting just the right shot of almost two dozen documents that you're going to see today—and by "we" I mean Benoît. I still have vivid images of him, balancing on one foot, halfway up the step ladder, aiming his camera down on the dining room table where we were laying out, one by one, all the things we wanted you to see today.

Thanks to Benoît's photography, you'll see for yourselves how the puzzle comes together. I'm sure that, like me, you'll be surprised and struck by the irony that the mystery of this murder turned out to be solved right here in our archives. In fact, the diary, the missing piece to the puzzle, has been sitting in the archives for quite a few years.

So, thanks to Benoît and the wonders of technology, we have the solution to the entire mystery right here on this little memory stick, which I am going to plug in here to this laptop.

So, thank you Shawn for the technical support, and thank you Benoît, and I also want to say thank you to the ladies of the Women's Guild here at St. Andrew's. I'm not a tea drinker, but the coffee was perfect, as were all those sweets—the brownies and the squares and the homemade doughnuts and everything else—absolutely scrumptious. Thank you, Ladies.

Oops! I better not drop this microphone. I don't often have to use one of these things. And I don't find myself in front of a crowd this size very often either. As you can probably imagine, as archivist of the Richmond County Historical Society, I toil largely in solitude. I do get emails and phone calls—sometimes from as far away as California, and I once got a call from Australia—and several times a year I will have a visitor arrive at the Archives.

Usually this is someone trying to fill in branches on a family tree, or a recently retired couple who are looking for information on the late-nineteenth-century farmhouse they bought somewhere nearby that they are about to start renovating.

Of course, it would be difficult to accommodate more than one or two visitors to the Archives at any one time. As those of you who are members of the Society know, it's not a very big space, something like twenty feet by fourteen. No doubt it was big enough for its original purpose. A hundred and fifty years ago, when what's now our museum was the Rectory of St. Andrew's Presbyterian Church, what's now the Archives was the summer kitchen. From late spring to early fall, it was where the minister's wife, or perhaps his housekeeper, would prepare meals over a hot, wood-burning stove. The heat was largely contained within the summer kitchen so that the rest of the house remained cooler. In the fall, of course, the stove would be moved back into the main kitchen so that, as it kept the soup simmering, it also warmed the house.

Those of you who've been to the Archives know that besides being rather small, the room is also—how can I put this?— let's say, quite full. Over the last sixty years, the Society has acquired—and continues to acquire—a wide variety of arte-facts and archival materials: books, papers, photographs, legal documents. Everything has to be catalogued and then stored on shelves and in cupboards and filing cabinets. There's not much elbow room. In fact, although I generally work at my desk, at times I have to gather up the materials I'm working on and appropriate the dining room table where I can spread all my papers out. In fact, if it weren't for the dining room table, I don't know where we could have shot all the photographs we did.

All of this to say I'm not accustomed to talking to a large crowd like this, and I'll try not to drop the microphone. Oops! Or knock over my glass of water here.

As Margaret said a moment ago, today's talk is about the Melbourne Murder, a crime that was never solved. You've all come this afternoon to hear about an act that none of us would ever commit. At least I think that no one here would ever commit . . .

I'm just joking, of course.

And yet, even though it's an act none of us would ever commit, it's an act that holds a great fascination for us. If you look around, you'll see that the church hall is practically full this afternoon. We're all here because we're fascinated by murder. We're appalled by it, of course, and we don't condone it in any way, and yet we're inevitably curious about it.

As Margaret pointed out, it is the *why* of a murder that most fascinates us. Why was someone's life brought to a sudden, violent end? Often, if the why is known, the police can more quickly find the *who*, the perpetrator of the murder. The other details are also clues that can potentially point to the murderer, who, if caught, will certainly be asked, "Why?"

The victim can almost always be identified, and when the story is reported, his, or her, identity is often one of the first things we learn. Similarly, we almost always know where the crime was committed, and generally when it was committed as well. Nor are we often left in the dark as to how it was committed, another detail that fascinates us. As a species, humans frequently display a morbid curiosity about the *how* of a murder, even if the details sometimes disturb us viscerally: a pipe wrench to the head, a piano wire around the throat, an ice pick through the heart, not to mention the more gruesome means of murder that have been tried, either in life or in fiction. It's part of the fascination of murder.

We're interested in all the details: How did a specific site come to be chosen by the murderer? Or, for that matter, how did the victim's presence in a particular place lead to his, or her, sudden death? What happened in the moments—or months—before the crime was committed? And what happened after?

We want to accumulate all those details. We want to collect them, one by one, and lay them out like a deck of tarot cards in order to reveal the big unknown: the why of the murder.

We are sapient creatures and our minds always seek an explanation, a logical construct. Our well-being rests to a large extent on our ability to make sense of the world around us. If something—even something as horrific as murder—happens for a reason that we can identify, then it becomes understandable, even if it remains unacceptable. If there's an explanation, we feel our feet are back on stable, solid ground. We want things to be logical, even if, as in the case of murder, the logic is warped or twisted logic. Mystery makes us uncomfortable.

The murder I'm going to talk about this afternoon—the murder on the Orford Mountain Railway—has remained an unsolved mystery for over a century. The perpetrator was never discovered, nor was a plausible reason for the murder ever put forward. The who and the why of the murder remained perplexing problems as long as the murder remained in the collective consciousness of the good citizens of Melbourne Township and the surrounding area. Those of us with an interest in local history know at least a little about the Melbourne Murder mostly because it's mentioned in *Richmond Now & Then*, a book that I imagine almost everyone has read by now.

For us, the murder is one of those darker spots on the canvas of our local history. Our past has something sacred about it, something we want to see in a glorious and heroic light. As we know—again from *Richmond Now & Then*—while we can be justifiably proud of the struggles and accomplishments of the early settlers—and some of you are their direct descendants—not every act was noble in intent. The Melbourne Murder falls into that category, along with Elmore Cushing's probable perjury at the trial of David McLane in Quebec City in 1797, or the attempt on the life of Francis Noel Annance, one of the last of the Abenaki, half a century later.

The murder of young Ralph Andosca was a tragedy. Identifying a perpetrator and proposing a motive—especially at this late date—will not lessen the tragedy. It's very much an academic exercise to review the facts today—over one hundred years later—and offer an answer to the question, Why? It's not the kind of revelation that's going to make the evening news. The murderer has long since gone to meet his maker, and those who would have had closure to see the perpetrator brought to justice are similarly long since interred.

Still, history has its own fascination—especially if you're a member of a historical society, as many of you are.

As you'll see for yourselves in just a minute, our answer to the question why?—why was this twelve-year-old murdered?—might possibly fall just short of the kind of factual evidence that a public prosecutor would want to present in court: fingerprints on the weapon, a credible eye witness, an irrefutable DNA match. Still, it's a possible and plausible answer; circumstantial evidence is sometimes sufficient to convince a jury to convict.

There are several threads that have to be pulled together and I'll ask you to be patient with me because it will take a few minutes to unfurl each one. But before we get into those threads, let me start with the murder itself. Let me show you, on the screen here, how we likely would have learned of the Melbourne Murder if we had been here, right where we are now, in the summer of 1905.

Especially in small communities such as ours, news spreads by word of mouth with remarkable rapidity, so there's no doubt that—had we been here in August of 1905—many of us would have heard what happened on the Orford Mountain Railway construction site from a neighbour or a friend. Still, that neigh-

14

bour or friend, like several others of us, would have learned of the murder when we picked up our copy of the *Sherbrooke Daily Record* and looked at the front page.

Does this remote work? Yes, there it is on the screen, the front page story from the Thursday, August 17, 1905, edition of the *Sherbrooke Daily Record*.

Chapter 2

Boy Shot Down In Cold Blood

Another Boy Murder, This Time At The Construction Camp

Of The O.M.R., A Few Miles From Windsor Mills

12-Year-Old Italian Lad Victim

Shot From Horse By Unknown Italian—May Have Been
In Revenge For Grievance Against Father—Murderer Has
Escaped—High Constable Moe And Coroner Bachand
Investigating

Windsor Mills, Aug. 17 (Special)—Drake Andosca, an
Italian lad, 12 years of age, was shot down in cold blood
last evening at the Orford Mountain Railway construction
camp some three miles from here.

While not as brutal in its details as the Farnham tragedy, the killing of the defenceless Italian boy is quite as
difficult to explain, anything like a motive being absent.

The boy was a son of Frank Andosca, who runs the
canteen at the camp. This man has several sons working
in the camp. The victim is the next to the youngest. He
was an errand boy at the camp.

Six o'clock had sounded and work was over for the
day. The boy was on a horse which had been unhitched
from a cart, and he was proceeding along the road toward
the stable. The horse belonged to Mr. James Todd.

At the moment of the shooting, the Todd boy was the only one in position to witness the attack. He, however, was in front and did not actually see the shooting, but he heard the repost, turned and saw an Italian disappearing in the bushes.

It appears that as the lad passed along the road, the murderer stepped from cover at the side and, levelling a gun in absolute cold blood, without a word, shot down the youth. The bullet or shot passed through the boy's body in the vicinity of his heart. He fell from the horse dead. The Todd boy turned just in time to see a man, an Italian, disappearing into the woods. The men of the construction gang, hearing the shot hastened to the spot. The little fellow was carried into camp but life was extinct.

The murderer was not immediately pursued. The Italians were not inclined to rush into the woods unarmed in an effort to capture one who had so callously shot down a young boy.

In the evening news of the affair was brought to Windsor. The coroner at Sherbrooke was notified as were also police and detective authorities at different points.

Why was the deed done? is a question which all are attempting to answer. Some believe that the murderer entertained some grievance against Frank Andosca and sought revenge through his son. This seems to be the only plausible theory.

The boy had no money and as far as the boy himself was concerned there could have been no incentive for a man of most desperate and reckless character to raise a weapon against him. The father's position was such, however, that certain of the Italians may have felt that they had a grievance. The ways of the Italian desperado are peculiar and it is not improbable that the boy was shot as a means of striking at the father.

Desperate Lot

These foreigners engaged in railway construction are a desperate lot. There are about a hundred on the OMR. Scarcely a day passes without a fight amongst themselves. These fights are not of the Canadian variety. Their temperament has not changed under the cooler atmosphere of Canada. And injury, imagined or real, instantly fills them with a desire for revenge. Their anger does not subside with the going down of the sun. It is nursed day by day. The opportunity to get even is patiently and sullenly awaited. A week or a month or more may pass. But sooner or later the victim will receive a blow, probably in the back, likely at night. He may not see his assailant but he can safely figure that someone is paying old scores.

And so it is believed that yesterday's murder was committed by someone who had perhaps waited a long time and failed to secure an opportunity to strike the father.

Paymaster Has Guard

The paymaster went through the OMR camp, yesterday, and paid the men. He took no chances.

He was accompanied by eight men in four teams. All, to use a common expression, were armed to the teeth. They carried Winchester rifles and revolvers. These firearms were in sight and must have been quite impressive.

Coroner and High Constable

Coroner, Dr. Bachand, and High Constable Moe proceeded to Windsor from Sherbrooke at 9:00 a.m. The coroner and the High Constable proceeded to the scene of the shooting to make preliminary investigations.

An inquest will be opened today.

Let me just turn this off for a minute. Here it is. No. OK! There we go. The screen is off.

I think I heard one or two little gasps of surprise a minute ago as you read this newspaper account. I think that I reacted the same way the first time I saw a newspaper from that era. The *Sherbrooke Daily Record* of 1905 looks very different compared to the paper today. As you saw, there was no front page photo, whereas today, there's always a colour photo, as often as not, taking up three-quarters of the front page. You also noticed that, even with the story of the Melbourne Murder taking up a third of the page, quite a number of other stories still made front-page news. They came, as you noticed from the headlines, from far and wide: King Goes to Austria—An Outing for the Benefit of His Health; Child Struck By Mowing Machine—Sad Accident on a Birchton Farm; Collision Near Cleveland, 12 Persons Killed and 25 Injured.

Clearly, unlike today when different sections of the paper are given over to particular topics like sports or politics, there seemed to be no distinction in 1905 between international news and local news.

On the topic of headlines, you all noticed that the headlines in 1905 pretty well told the entire story. Today of course, they're generally kept as short as possible. If you glance at the tabloids at the supermarket checkout (and I hope I'm not the only one to do that), you see lots of headlines that are no more than one or two words long: Elvis Lives, UFO Sighting.

You probably also noticed that, unlike today when *Record* reporters—like reporters everywhere and in all media—put their names to their stories, there wasn't a single story with a byline back in 1905.

All of that is perhaps superficial, interesting differences to note, but not really significant. When I first read that story, what most shocked me was the unrestrained racism that fills almost a quarter of the article. "These foreigners are a desperate lot," is a line that we recognize today as being racist and xenophobic. We would like to think that these are sentiments that have been eradicated from our society, and as long as we don't look too hard, we would be right. We certainly don't expect that kind of racism in the morning paper, nor are we accustomed to seeing it directed towards Italians. Of course, those of you who've read a bit of history know that, both in the United States and in Canada, prejudice against Italians at the time was quite pronounced. Canada was staunchly British, and Italians were foreigners who spoke a foreign language. As bad, they were Papists—Catholics rather than Anglicans. By and large, as new immigrants, they were generally poor. That being said, at the time, there was also considerable prejudice against other immigrant groups as well. The Irish, the Jews, and the Chinese were all guilty of not being British—and so were the French Canadians. This prejudice was as virulent here in the Townships as anywhere else in the country, I might add.

I imagine that some of you also found that both the graphic details and the breathless tone of the story serve to make it unabashedly sensationalist.

But the detail that I want to start with is the way the story of the Melbourne Murder was sandwiched between two other stories: the recent murder of a boy in Farnham mentioned at the beginning and the description of the paymaster's monthly visit to the work camp at the end.

Why there are three stories in this one article is a valid question. Neither of the two others has any direct bearing on the Melbourne murder, but both would have been very relevant to us if we'd been here in the summer of 1905.

In fact, if we had been here back in 1905, just three days before reading about the killing of young Andosca on the

Orford Mountain Railway, we would have read this on the front page of the Monday, August 14 edition of the *Sherbrooke Daily Record*.

Oops! That's the wrong button. Here it is:

Chapter 3

Foul Murder At Farnham, Que

14 Year-Old Boy Found In Lumber Yard Near
Station With Brains Battered Out
By Stone
Mystery Surrounds The Tragedy

Lad Went Out On Errand Early Sunday Morning—Tramp
Or Drunken Fiend?—Detective McCaskill on Case—
Coroner Mitchell Begins Inquest—Some Suspicions—
No Arrest Yet

Farnham Aug 14—(Special)—Farnham was the scene
of a foul and bloody murder late Saturday night or early
Sunday morning.
The victim is the 14 year-old son of Mr. E. Audette the
Secretary-Treasurer of the town.
The murderer or murderers are still unknown, and the
motive for the horrible deed is a mystery.
The discovery that a murder had been committed was
first made about eleven o'clock, Sunday morning, when
a couple of men were passing by a short cut through the
lumberyard of Messers A.B. Comeau & Co. (next to the
Central Vermont freight yards).
There they found the stiff and lifeless body of the
young lad lying in a pool of blood.
The body was face-down, with the head all battered
in, and near-by, a large stone weighing six or seven

pounds, covered with blood and hair, evidently the instrument of death.

So great had been the force of the blow which killed him, that his head was driven several inches into the ground.

The lad who was employed by the C.P.R. as night call-boy at the round-house, was on duty at the time, and was on his way to call an engineer and fireman for a train when he met his untimely end.

His lantern was found about sixty feet away from his body, showing that he must have had a first struggle and run some distance before being struck down.

There was great excitement about town when news of the murder reached the ears of the public. And as the brutal nature of the crime became known, indignation was great. It would not have fared well with the perpetrator had he fallen into the hands of the excited crowd which soon assembled near the scene of the crime

McCaskill Called

The Montreal detective authorities were communicated with and Detective McCaskill arrived here about six o'clock last night on a C.P.R. freight. High Constable Boisvert also came down from Cowansville.

The Coroner of the district was also notified and this morning opened an inquest.

The detective apparently had little to work upon.

Motive Lacking

Motive for such a crime seemed entirely lacking.

They examined the body of the victim and the spot where the crime occurred. Here was the body of a young lad. His head had been battered by a rock until life was extinct. The boy was last seen at one a.m. He had left to perform the duties of his position, crossing the lonely yard in the early hours of the morning. He had no money or is supposed to have had none. He certainly could have had no enemy, the boy of 14 years. Who could be lying in wait for such a young victim?

No motive for the deliberate and dastardly crime offered itself to the detectives.

Detective McCaskill however has a theory. He is working it out and an arrest may be soon made. He had not divulged his views.

Public Theory

The public has discussed the matter in all its details. They, also, have a theory. They say it must have been the act of some man who had been converted into a fiend by drink and who in his frenzy had struck down the lad as he passed. Or, possibly, some tramp, with desperate tendency, thinking the boy had money attacked him.

It is thought by some that murder may not have been the first intention of the assailants. As already stated the boy dropped his lantern some distance from the spot where he was struck down. The assassin may have attempted to seize him, and failing, hurled a stone after the fleeing lad, which struck him down; then to stifle the cries and hide his crime, the fiend may again have applied the rock, driving the lad's head into the earth.

These are some of the explanations which offer themselves.

Let me turn this off again for a second.

This was the news that people in Melbourne Township had woken up to on Monday, just three days before they learned that young Andosca was killed. That a boy had been murdered in Farnham was horrific for a couple of reasons. First, because we assume that normally death is for the old; young people are

24

not supposed to die, and especially, they are not supposed to be so brutally murdered. Secondly, because Farnham was far too close to home. Farnham was here, in the Townships, not some heathen enclave in some barbaric corner of the world. More than that was the fact that Farnham, like Richmond, was a railway town, even if the CPR.station and rail yards were not quite as large or important as those of the Grand Trunk Railway that were here. The young victim was a railway employee, and he'd met his sudden end near a rail yard. Could something like that happen here as well?

For Farnham, as for Richmond and to a lesser extent for hundreds of other towns across the country, the presence of the railway was of significant economic importance, both for the community and for the surrounding area. Here, the GTR employed hundreds of men: train engineers, firemen, conductors, porters, baggage handlers, telegraph operators, ticket agents, security guards, and call boys. Because the roundhouse, where the big steam engines were maintained and repaired, was located here, there were several dozens more men employed as mechanics, machinists, blacksmiths, and labourers, along with several mechanical and hydraulic engineers for good measure. To the extent that Richmond lived up to the "rich" in its name, it was primarily due to the presence of the Grand Trunk Railway roundhouse and yards.

The financial rewards provided by the railway were appreciated, but the population was well aware that wealth came at a price. By way of illustration, let me put another small item from the *Sherbrooke Daily Record* up on the screen.

This short item appeared in the paper on Wednesday, August 16:

Met Horrible Death

Workman Hammered to a Pulp by Steam Hammer

Was Employed in G.T.R. Shops, Point St. Charles

Montreal, August 16 (Special)—Jaben Wass, an employee of the Grand Trunk shops at Point St. Charles, met a horrible death today, when he got caught under one of the steam hammers and before the machinery could be stopped he was literally hammered to a pulp. He was 50 years old.

Not that people here needed to be reminded of the occupational hazards of railway life, but the newspaper—like all newspapers at the time and our various media today—found it difficult to resist a tragic story. Bad news, for the media in general, is good news, in that it sells papers or keeps people glued to the screen.

With respect to the Farnham murder, the paper on August 16 carried a bit of good news. As you can see, the item was very short, consisting of no more than a headline. Here it is on the screen:

The Farnham Murder Case

Two Arrests Have Been Made—
Jos. Roy Held for Perjury and Possible
Suspect—Unknown Stranger Placed in Cells To-day Noon
By Detectives—Is Not Allowed to Talk—
Inquest Resumes To-morrow

This story, even if only in headline form, would have brought at least a slight sense of reassurance with respect to the murder of young Audette. Not that anyone would already have forgotten the graphic details of the fourteen-year-old's murder, but the news that the long arm of the law had already nabbed the perpetrators would have given the general public the beginning of a sense of closure, and certainly a sense of relief.

That same sense of closure would have come from the closing paragraphs of the story of the Andosca murder. The two short paragraphs that describe the paymaster's visit to the work camp are in reference to an earlier story that shook the good people of the area almost as much as the murder of August 17, the story of an attempted robbery.

Let me go back to the screen again. This is from the July 18, 1905 edition of the *Sherbrooke Daily Record*:

Shooting On Orford Mountain Railway

Desperados Attack Paymaster At Construction Camp Near Windsor Mills—Seriously Wound Him And Shoot His Horse Dead

Oops! What did I do? What happened there? What do I have to do to get the screen back? Let me just try this. No, that's not right. I'm sorry about that. Shawn? Shawn are you still here somewhere? I need technical support. Oh, good. No, I think that's the button I pushed.

While Shawn sorts out all the electronics let me briefly summarize what you would have read for yourselves if the screen hadn't died on us.

But, let me give you a little bit of background first.

The Orford Mountain Railway was a short line that had been in operation, at this point, for about a decade. It ran from Eastman to Kingsbury, or perhaps we should say from Kingsbury to Eastman because it was primarily a freight line and much of that freight consisted of goods—primarily wood products like lumber, cedar shakes, and butter boxes—being shipped from Kingsbury to Eastman where they were transferred onto other trains belonging to the Canadian Pacific Railway.

The OMR had been started by Judge Samuel Foster, and in 1905 he was proceeding with the construction of the first of two spurs. This first spur, the one where the murder occurred, was to extend the OMR line from Kingsbury to Greenlay, situated across the St. Francis River from Windsor. This spur would create a link of sorts between the nation's two most important rail lines, the Grand Trunk, which ran through Windsor, and the Canadian Pacific which ran through Eastman. Judge Foster foresaw interesting potential in this link, well worth the financial risk associated with twelve miles of track.

The project had not been without its setbacks, but I'll say a little more about that later on. For the time being, suffice it to say that there were about a hundred men employed in this endeavour. The construction workers were divided up into several crews, most consisting of a dozen men or more, working at different sites along the line. They were paid monthly and they were paid in cash.

This meant that once a month the Orford Mountain Railway's paymaster, a man by the name of Charles Percy, would withdraw bills and coins totalling about seventeen thousand dollars from the Eastern Townships Bank on St. Georges Street in Windsor, pack the money into saddlebags, and ride to the different construction sites to pay each worker individually.

Percy normally worked out of the OMR offices located in Eastman but on paydays he and his son would travel by train from Eastman to Sherbooke, then from Sherbrooke to Windsor where they visited the bank to pick up their cash and then rented horses to complete their trip out to the work sites.

Their ride grew a little longer every month because the crews were working progressively further away from Greenlay and closer to Kingsbury. Originally, the work had been started at both ends—Greenlay and Kingsbury—but because of events I'll explain a little later, at the time of the murder, all of the work was being done from the Greenlay end, the men leapfrogging their way south-west in increments of an eighth of a mile. Following the lines set by surveyors two summers before, the crews first had to cut down trees to create a swath thirty-two feet wide. Then the ground would have to be cleared, before being levelled, and then built up with layers of sand and gravel that would make the subgrade, the solid base needed to support the ballast, ties, and rails that would eventually make up the train tracks.

While the trips for the paymaster grew progressively longer with every payday, he had an exceptionally good road to ride on, and one with no traffic.

On July 16, towards four o'clock in the afternoon, Percy and his son were making their way along the rail bed towards the first camp when two armed men stepped out of the woods and demanded the payroll. Percy and his son grabbed their saddlebags, leapt from their horses, and ran away from their attackers and into the woods. The would-be robbers fired at their fleeing victims. Percy's left shoulder was grazed by a bullet, and the horse he'd rented was killed by another bullet, but the paymaster and his son made good their escape, without losing a penny of the company payroll, it must be added.

The two attackers, just as in the case of the murder a month later, were identified by the paper as Italians. They panicked, turned, and fled. Moments later, construction workers, alerted by the gun shots, came running from further up the rail bed carrying their picks and shovels. Percy and his son, despite the dead horse and the superficial wound, continued on with their task of paying out the men's monthly wages.

Charles Percy seems not to have been too badly shaken by the attempted robbery, and his arrival the following month accompanied by eight heavily armed men was likely not entirely his idea, and probably done as much for show as for security.

All of this to say that, even before the murder of young Andosca, the summer of 1905 had been at least a little alarming for people in the area. The senseless slaughter of an innocent twelve-year old in broad daylight had just served to prove the adage that things come in threes. *Jamais deux sans trois,* as we say in French. Local news was becoming as dark as international news. The same day the Andosca murder was reported, the *Sherbrooke Daily Record* ran stories about a riot that killed sixteen people in the Russian city of Novgorod and an update on the war raging between Russia and Japan. Although anyone who read the paper in its entirety also learned that William Hall of Knowlton celebrated his eightieth birthday with family in Bolton Glen, and that the temperature this month was fluctuating wildly: in Sherbrooke it was one degree above freezing in the early morning but reached a high of 87°F in the shade later on the same afternoon.

Chapter 4

Windsor did not have a municipal police force in 1905, and the closest thing to law enforcement was the railway police stationed ten miles up the track in Richmond. While these men wore uniforms and inspired a certain amount of fear and respect, they constituted little more than a private security service and their legal authority went no further than the property lines of the Grand Trunk Railway. They were able enough to keep most hobos out of empty rail cars, and prevent most boys from repeating the experiment of laying coins on the track too many times. However, a murder case, especially one on property belonging to a rival—or at least a different—railway, was as far beyond their competence as it was beyond their jurisdiction. When a call was eventually made to the police, some two hours after the shooting, it was to the police force in Sherbrooke.

It's easy to imagine the events that unfolded in the moments after the gunshot that took young Andosca's life.

Richard Todd, a fourteen-year-old already doing a man's work, was seated on a wagon being pulled by two draft horses. He was no more than ten or twelve yards in front of the Andosca boy, and he swivelled around the moment he heard the blast. What he saw was Ralph Andosca throw up his arms and lurch forward over his horse's shoulder, even as the horse, startled by the noise, bolted. The horse, a small, sturdy Canadian, was being ridden bare back so that Ralph's body toppled easily and unimpeded to the ground, while the horse, startled by the blast, took only a few quick steps before it calmed down and stopped right behind the familiar wagon. What Richard Todd also saw was a figure, holding a long gun, stepping smartly into the woods. Within a second or two the figure had disappeared.

Richard Todd dropped the reins, jumped off the wagon, and ran to Ralph Andosca's lifeless body. For a moment, he was too startled to do any more than stand over the corpse. As he tried to decide what to do, he was conscious of several things at the same time. If Ralph had been shot, then so too could he be shot, although the figure he had seen had been moving away very quickly. Viscerally, he didn't feel himself to be in any danger, but he knew he had to do more than just stand over the slain boy. He was about four miles from home. He was conscious of the eighty-three dollars and fifty cents that he had in his pockets—money for work that he and his father had done for the railway (mostly hauling sand and gravel) plus money for the use of their horses and wagon for several days. He would definitely feel safer putting the money on the kitchen table, even as he told his father and mother about the shooting.

But help in the form of the construction crew was far closer, around a slight curve and less than half a mile to the nearest work site where a few men could likely still be found. It was just after six in the evening, and the work day was officially over, but there was still work going on. The problem was that going back towards the work site meant passing the spot where the shooter had disappeared into the woods. With the money he had in his pockets, he was conscious of being a target for anyone with criminal intent.

Still, the shooter—someone dressed in dark pants and a lighter coloured shirt, someone wearing a hat and half-running with a long gun in one hand—was unmistakably running away. Had the shooter wanted to kill him as well, Richard reasoned, he would have been as easy a target as the young Italian.

Richard's first thought was to ignore the wagon; if the hitched horses continued on without him, they would make their way home. But some other instinct prompted him to hobble the horses. If they moved it would not be more than a few feet. He mounted the Canadian, turned it back towards the way it had come, and urged the horse to a quick canter, as fast a pace as the old horse could achieve, and rushed back up the sub grade towards the work site.

He didn't go far at all before he saw half a dozen men hurrying towards him with picks and shovels in their hands.

"Andosca's son has been killed," he told them.

"No!" the men cried in disbelief. "How? Why?"

"We must let Andosca know," said one of the men. "I can go," and he turned to go back the way he had come.

"Take the horse," Richard told him, "it'll be faster." The man nodded his thanks, took the reins, mounted the small horse and set off at a quick canter.

The others dropped their tools and, with Richard, quick marched towards the spot where Ralph Andosca's body stretched lifeless on the ground.

No one touched the body. They stared, dumbfounded, at the boy's blood-stained back. They were all Catholics and almost unconsciously they crossed themselves and mumbled a prayer for his departed soul. Then they stood, milling about, asking Richard to repeat his story, to describe what had happened, what he had seen.

As they stood waiting, Richard wondered about continuing his trek home. His father, he knew, would appreciate another pair of hands to help with the evening chores. He was also aware that his mother too would be a little anxious to see him home with the month's wages. There were the horses as well that would be glad to get back to the stable for some cold water and a feed of oats. There was nothing more he could do than just stand there; and yet, he felt that it wouldn't be right to leave, not until someone could relieve him of the responsibility he felt towards Ralph Andosca, even if the boy was dead, perhaps especially because he was dead.

Frank Andosca arrived less than twenty minutes later, still wearing his cook's apron, riding the old Canadian. With him was the foreman, Cyril Ashenden, riding his own horse, a big roan that could have easily outpaced the small Canadian, but Ashenden was clearly keeping his animal in check, staying just behind the camp cook.

"*Figlio mio!*" the cook cried as he stumbled off his horse and fell over the body of his lifeless son.

Ashenden dismounted and held himself back for a minute, as if paying the slain boy his respects with a moment of silence. He then moved towards Richard Todd who was standing quietly with the construction crew several feet back from the murdered boy, although just a little apart from them; not only younger than the others, but also noticeably not of their fraternity, his clothes his own, not the uniform blue overalls of the Italians; his face less haggard, his hands not as encrusted with grime and dirt.

"What happened?" Ashenden asked.

Richard Todd described how Ralph Andosca had been following his wagon and team, how a shot had suddenly rung out, how he'd seen Ralph pitch forward, fatally shot, and how he'd caught a glimpse of a figure, armed with a long gun, disappearing into the woods.

"Show me where," Ashenden asked.

"You see there, to the right, that pile of branches and rubble, he disappeared behind that."

"Probably where he was waiting for you," Ashenden said, as much to himself as to the boy. "You didn't see him, I suppose, as you passed by."

"No, I didn't see anybody."

"A man planning an ambush couldn't ask for much better to remain hidden," Ashenden reflected as he stepped around the large pile of debris.

"I'm sorry you had to experience this," the foreman said to Richard. "I hope it doesn't stay with you too long. I'd like to keep your father's wagon and team for another hour or so. We'll feed and water the horses at the cook camp and I'll have two men bring them back to you this evening. They shouldn't be very long. You take your horse and go on home now. Your folks might start worrying if you're too much longer."

"Thank you, sir," said Richard, surprised at the sense of relief that washed over him so suddenly and unexpectedly that he felt tears welling up behind his eyes. Without looking at anyone, he crossed over to where the Canadian stood waiting, took the reins, mounted the horse, and turned the animal towards home at a brisk walking pace.

Ashenden waited until Frank Andosca stood up before approaching the grieving man with his hand outstretched.

"*Mi spiace tanto, Andosca.*"

"*Ma, perché?*" the cook asked in a barely audible voice, his eyes red, his face wet with tears.

"I don't know," Ashenden answered, his face drawn with worry. "I don't know and I'm very sorry."

There was grief on Ashenden's face but some of the furrows on his brow were due to worry as much as to grief.

As best they could, using their forearms as brooms, the men cleaned the wagon bed and gently laid the boy's body down, his head facing forward and resting on Frank Andosca's apron, folded to make the semblance of a pillow. Frank Andosca sat with the driver, and even though there would have been room for the other men to ride on the wagon, they all walked, as if in a procession, behind the improvised hearse.

Ashenden turned his horse in the opposite direction and urged the animal to a canter. His horse was fresh, and the rail bed solid and smooth, and he could have galloped the four miles to Grand Trunk Railway station in Windsor, but he had a lot to think about, and the extra time would be good for him, and any delay would make no difference to the young boy being carted in the opposite direction.

Chapter 5

Aside from the grief he felt for his cook's great loss, a loss with which he could relate only too easily, Ashenden had another reason to feel overwhelmed. He now had a great deal to worry about. Accidents—sometimes minor, but other times resulting in serious injury, and even death—were an accepted condition of any major construction project. Ashenden always hoped not to lose anyone, but it was always in the back of his mind that he might at any time lose one or more men to an accident. While the shooting was anything but an accident, the sudden death of Ralph Andosca represented the most serious personnel loss imaginable for Ashenden. He now had a very serious problem that had to be solved as quickly as possible.

Yet, he seemed unable to concentrate, to focus his mind on the problem at hand. His mind's eye kept going back to the bloodstained body of Ralph Andosca, to the tearstained face of the dead boy's father. The images provoked a physical pain, as if a giant hand had clamped on his visceral organs and was now slowly twisting them, wrenching them out of his body by their roots. He was unable to keep his shoulders back and his spine straight, and he rode half-bent in the saddle, the reins clutched to his stomach as if to keep his innards from spilling out.

Despite having been born with more advantages than most, Ashenden's journey through life had not been without its share of tragedy. He was the youngest child and only son of a British diplomat and a Piedmontese countess, although by the time he was born, in 1867, the country in which she had been nobly born had ceased to exist, having ceded its autonomy towards the creation of a united Italy.

He was several years younger than his sisters and enjoyed a cosseted childhood spent in considerable comfort in three different European capitals. He spent a few of his childhood summers with his paternal grandparents at their ancestral home near Grantham, but others he spent with his mother's family in Volpiano, near Turin. He was tutored at home although it was always understood that, when he turned thirteen, he would, as his father had, attend the expensive Repton Public School in Derbyshire. This was in fact a private school but its purpose was to prepare young men to enter public service and fill bureaucratic roles in government. He was an active child, imaginative and manually dextrous; he took pleasure in solving puzzles and in building things.

The summer Cyril turned eleven he was in the room when his father gave a sudden start, clutched at his chest, and dropped dead of a heart attack. With his mother and Sandra, the youngest of his three sisters, he moved into a small manor house near Grantham, less than two miles from Ashenden Hall that he had known as a child and that was now the property of his least favourite uncle. It was a difficult adjustment for the diminished family. The lively social life that was an integral part of diplomatic service had suddenly been replaced by the quiet of rural England. The many perks that came with ambassadorships evaporated overnight.

His mother was lonely, even more so after Sandra married and left home just a year after her father's death. She had loved her husband dearly, and had always considered herself close to his family; but now that he was gone, so too was the bond to his family. Then there was the climate; she found England cold, damp, and dark. Two years after she became a widow, she sold the house in Grantham and moved back to Volpiano to look after her aging and ailing mother.

Cyril spent that summer in Italy, where he saw his mother regain some of the colour and vitality that had been washed out of her in the Derbyshire countryside. But he was thirteen, and at the end of the summer, alone, he travelled by train and steamer back to England to start school.

He had no experience of classroom settings nor of dormitory life. The public school that he had grown up believing to be a mystical, magical place turned out to be anything but. He found himself wearing a uniform that was uncomfortable and looked foolish. The food was atrocious. The masters, with a single exception, were stern, unsmiling figures who were dull, uninspiring pedants.

In the middle of his second week at Repton, at the end of class, he was told to report to the Headmaster's office where, for the offence of having passed a spare nib to the boy beside him, he received three vicious swats of the cane across his backside. Four days after that, he was roused from his bed and told to report downstairs to the seniors' room. There he found half a dozen senior boys including Hibbins, to whom he had been assigned as a fag, a personal servant. Hibbins was swishing a long, thin cane, like that of the headmaster. As had the Headmaster, Hibbins thrashed him. His transgression, he was told, was that he had been slow to fetch fresh apparel for Hibbins from the laundry room. He explained that the tardiness was in no way his fault, but to no avail. Worse than the pain was the humiliation.

Two days later, under the cover of darkness, thirteen-year old Cyril Ashenden crept out of his dormitory, made his way downstairs where he climbed out of a ground floor window, and escaped from one of England's more prestigious public schools.

Some forty hours later, dishevelled, tired, and hungry, he turned up at Ashenden Hall, where he received scant sympathy and none at all from his father's older brother. "That's simply not done, my boy," the uncle said. "Roberts will drive you back first thing tomorrow morning." With that, he was dismissed. He bore the avuncular coldness in stoic silence, his features passive but his mind already racing ahead to other alternatives, for the one thing he would not be doing was returning to Repton.

His aunt took enough pity on him that he was given his supper, although he was made to eat it alone in a small storage room off the pantry. Similarly, there was no question of his sleeping in the room that he had always slept in as a child. Rather he was put in the hands of the housekeeper who was told to find a bed for him somewhere in the servants' quarters.

Ashenden Hall had a staff of over a dozen, and it so happened that one of the footmen had been give three days leave to go home for his mother's funeral. Moved by a combination of practicality and indecision, the housekeeper gave Cyril the footman's room for the night. It was easier to put him in that bed than to take out a cot and get new sheets and blankets. As well, the housekeeper, who had been with the family a long time, and who knew Cyril, was a little confused by a situation of which she'd been told nothing, and was uncertain how complicit she should be in adding to the boy's humiliation. The footman's was a relatively nice room—as servants' quarters went—and giving it to the boy was her way of mitigating the punishment to which he was being subjected.

For the second time in three nights, thirteen-year old Ashenden fled under cover of darkness. He left the ancestral home in ill-fitting clothes and with almost five pounds in cash. He left a short note for the footman explaining that he had to borrow from him, and that he would shortly repay the loan with interest. In fact, three months later, the footman, who rarely received mail, got an envelope from abroad in which he found a bank draft for ten pounds; he told no one, keeping as quiet as he had when he returned from his mother's funeral to find some of his clothes and all of his savings gone and an enigmatic note in their place.

It took Ashenden just over two months to get to his grandmother's house in Piedmont, walking most of the way. He arrived unkempt and bedraggled; thinner, tougher, and wiser than the schoolboy who had been sent off to boarding school a scant six weeks before. Even to his mother, he was almost unrecognizable.

In that time his mother had received a total of three letters from the school, each shorter than the previous one, and none bearing any more information than the first, that her son had disappeared. For her part she had written the headmaster any number of times, and had also had a brief and fruitless exchange of letters with her brother-in-law.

Through her solicitor, she requested a refund of school fees from Repton. This was granted after the briefest of negotiations.

Cyril was sent to a *liceo* in Turin, a public school that was in all ways the exact opposite of the public school he'd fled in England. (First and foremost, it was not a private school like Repton back in Derbyshire but a public school as we understand the term here.)

During the week, he stayed with a family in Turin who provided him with room and board. On Saturday afternoons, after a half day of classes, he returned to his grandmother's home in Volpiano. Within a few weeks he was socially settled in his new environment. Academically, from the beginning, he thrived.

Four years later he enrolled at the University of Padua where he opted to study civil engineering. At times, the mathematics involved was a little challenging, but he was assiduous, and determined, and he responded doggedly to the problems he was set. On the other hand, he went through his physics texts as if they were entertaining novels. When he graduated in 1886, at the age of twenty-two, it was near the top of his class.

Armed with an engineering degree from one of the oldest universities in Europe, he found work with relative ease. He spoke four languages; he was personable, as able to talk with crowds as to walk with kings. He could take orders without offense and give them without offending. He was thorough in his planning, competent and conscientious, and on occasion even artistic and imaginative in his designs.

On his twenty-ninth birthday, at an event to mark the opening of a new water treatment facility in Brussels, he met Emily Richardson and two years later they were married.

Perhaps ironically, Emily was from near Nottingham, and while she didn't know the Ashendens, she knew the name, Ashenden Hall being less than twenty miles from her home in Radcliffe on Trent. Her father was an industrialist, a manufacturer of valves and pumps, a number of which had found their way into the Brussels water supply system.

In the spring of 1903, Ashenden was finishing up work on an extension to Bristol's sewage system. It was to be his last job as an engineer. After resisting for several years, he had accepted his father-in-law's invitation to come to work for him. Evan Richardson was seventy-four. He had been a widower for over two decades and he was conscious of his own slowly declining health.

He couldn't have been happier in his daughter's choice of a husband, for he saw in Cyril Ashenden the son he would have wanted to have, someone fully fit to continue in his footsteps, to continue the relatively lucrative manufacture and sales of industrial valves and pumps. He had waited only until his daughter and his new son-in-law were back from their honeymoon in Paris before proposing to Cyril that he join him in business.

He'd borne his son-in-law's initial reluctance with patience and had waited until the birth of his first granddaughter before raising the question again.

After the birth of his first son, Ashenden had agreed to his father-in-law's proposal. He would not join the firm immediately, for he had previous commitments he wanted to keep, but as soon as those were fulfilled he would join his father-in-law with a view to maintaining and perhaps even expanding the company's line of products, and leading the firm into the new century.

In anticipation of this change in their lives, he and Emily had bought a house, a century-old manor house on twelve acres of land less than two miles from the house in which she had grown up. They had started the task of modernizing the house to suit their needs and tastes, although with Cyril working, it was Emily who often found herself in charge of supervising the work at Hillview Hall.

In the meantime, for the duration of the Bristol project, the young family were renting a small but entirely suitable house just outside of Bristol.

On May 14, Emily along with three-year old Prudence and one-year old Peter, bid Cyril good-bye and boarded the train in Bristol. The three of them, accompanied by the nanny, were going to Northampton where they would spend three days with Emily's close friend, Rebecca Cartwright, before continuing on to Nottingham to evaluate progress on the house renovations.

Late in the afternoon of the 18th, Ashenden received a telegram. There had been a serious derailment on the London Midlands Railway line. A northbound passenger train had left the track injuring dozens and killing fourteen, among them Emily, Prudence, and Peter.

The accident had occurred less than five miles from Nottingham, and was blamed on the carelessness of the man at the throttle.

The day after the funerals, intrigued by some news he had heard—but not read—Ashenden made his way to the site of the accident where he found a large construction crew busy at work. From a distance, he studied the site for a long time. He took note in a cold and analytical way of the lay of the land with its folding hills, and the run of the rails on the long radius of the curve. In particular he noted the brook—wide but far from laying claim to the name of river—that drew rainwater from an extensive basin and that ran down to the tracks. He eventually came away convinced that the man at the throttle had not been the only engineer who had failed in his task.

What followed for Ashenden was a period during which he felt as if he and everything around him had been hollowed out. He walked about with the palm of his hand against his stomach to reassure himself that there was flesh where some sixth sense insisted there was only empty space. The manor house was a large, empty chamber of no use and no interest. When his father-in-law died only five months after Emily's death, Ashenden immediately took steps to sell the company, for he no longer needed to pretend an interest that had never fully taken root.

Job offers came to which he wrote polite refusals. He had no interest in solving the problems associated with bringing fresh water to urban centres, or the equally serious problem of delivering them of the black water they created, a field in which he had earned an enviable reputation.

The same day that he finished liquidating his assets in England, he arranged a trip to America. He had no idea where exactly he was going, but he knew he had to get away. The day before he sailed, in the lobby of the London hotel where he was staying, he struck up a casual conversation with a man who gave him a card with the name Belknap, and an address in Boston, written on it.

With a start, Ashenden realized that his horse had carried him almost to Greenlay. Whatever time he had had to find a solution had now passed. The problem was still there. Still, as he tried to straighten himself in the saddle, he knew that he would first call the police in Sherbrooke, and then he'd call Judge Foster. All the good news he'd reported to the judge earlier in the day would be for naught. He and the judge would have some important decisions to make.

Chapter 6

Ashenden was able to place a trunk call to the Sherbrooke police station just after seven thirty.

At the time, Sherbrooke's police station was located just off South Wellington Street, no more than a five-minute walk to the train station. Its eight officers were serving a population of some twenty thousand that was predominantly French speaking, even if English remained the lingua franca of commerce and politics.

It was Ashenden's good luck to speak to Roderick Moe, whose rank of high constable made him the second in command of the force. Moe was on day shift, but just happened to have stopped by the station that evening to check on a drunk that he'd jailed earlier in the day. Moe was next to the phone when it rang.

The high constable had Ashenden repeat his story slowly twice to make sure that he had fully understood. A young boy, a member of a large immigrant construction crew, had been shot in the back and killed on a railway construction site some three or four miles out of Windsor, but on the opposite side of the river in Melbourne Township.

"There's a northbound train leaving Sherbrooke at 8:50 a.m.," Moe told Ashenden. "It should be at Windsor station at 9:10. Can you have someone meet us there? I'll come with the coroner."

"I'll have a wagon for you," Ashenden assured him, "and if I can't be there myself, I'll have a man there to meet you."

He terminated the call and immediately asked the operator to put a second call through, again to Sherbrooke, but this time to the Three Forks Hotel. Could a message be got to Judge Foster to call him at the Windsor station as soon as possible?

He sat down to wait, hoping the judge might call back sooner rather than later. He was suddenly aware of his stomach reminding him that supper-time had come and gone, and he had not eaten.

He'd been sitting less than five minutes when the operator signalled him from the other side of the waiting room that his call had come through.

"Thank you for calling back, sir."

"I haven't had my coffee yet, Ashenden, I hope this won't take too long."

"I'm afraid it might, sir. I have bad news. Andosca's youngest boy was shot in the back and killed less than two hours ago."

"Good God, man! You're not serious!"

"I'm afraid so..."

"Andosca's youngest! That's the lad who brought us our coffee this afternoon. Seemed a very likeable lad. What is he, thirteen, fourteen? And he was shot? Killed? What happened?"

"He's twelve, sir. He's not on the payroll but he does help around the cook camp, and occasionally elsewhere. He's a useful boy. There's no explaining what happened. I sent him back with the Todd boy to return Todd's horses and wagon for the night. The lad enjoys riding a horse, and he can make the walk back to camp in an hour or so. It's something he's been doing all summer.

"I sent them off shortly after six. They hadn't gone far when someone stepped out of the woods and killed the boy. Shot him in the back with a shotgun at close range. This was close to Mile Four, near the wide curve."

"I assume that Andosca must know by now."

"He does. He saw the boy's body where he fell. He's since brought the body back to the cook camp."

"Why would anyone shoot the lad?"

"It's a wonder, sir, makes no sense at all."

"Have you contacted the police?"

"Just now, just before I called you. There's a high constable who will be here tomorrow, with a coroner. They're coming on the first train and should be here just after nine."

"Andosca's son! Good Lord! What is the world coming to? Andosca! Poor man! And poor us! This is going to put a real spanner in the works, Ashenden."

"Yes, sir, it certainly is."

"If there's one man we can't do without, it's Andosca. An army advances on its stomach, and the same is true for a construction crew."

"Yes, sir, that's what they say, and I couldn't agree more." Ashenden was aware that his words were just filling empty space. He knew what his employer was thinking, knew that the problem was as difficult for the judge to grapple with as it was for him; and Ashenden had been aware of it since he'd started his solitary ride into town.

"Andosca's going to have to bury his boy, and he'll want to bury him back home. That's only natural. Although, in this weather, it would be best to have the boy embalmed here. We'll cover the cost. See if you can't find a funeral parlour there in Greenlay or Windsor and make arrangements. Let them know that we'll pay."

"I'm sure I'll be able to find one, sir."

"We're going to be in a dilemma with Andosca."

"I'm afraid so, sir."

"We can't manage without a cook, but if we insist Andosca ship the body back home while he stays on the job, we'll run the risk of having the man quit on the spot. On the other hand, if we let him take the body back home for burial, we'll be without him for several days: one day's travel there and another day's travel back. At least a day, probably two, maybe more, to arrange for the funeral. That's five days. Where can we find a cook for five days?"

"A camp cook."

"You're right, Ashenden, a camp cook."

"A camp cook and kitchen crew as well. It's Andosca's sons who help their father, and I expect all of them will want to go back with the body."

"Yes. More's the pity. I thought I was doing well to get the entire kitchen crew from the same family. If someone else had been helping with the kitchen, we might have had someone able to step in for Andosca. Bad luck, as it turned out."

"Yes, sir, bad luck all the way around."

"All right, Ashenden. Let's do this one step at a time. Tomorrow morning first. We'll assume that Andosca will return to Albany with his boy, but he won't be able to leave first thing because the body has to be released by the coroner. What time did you say the police were coming?"

"The train comes in at 9:10, sir."

"Do you think Andosca can do breakfast tomorrow?"

"I would think so, sir. No doubt he'll be distraught, but I imagine he'll find it easier being busy with breakfast than just waiting for the coroner."

"I think so too. Still, we need someone to start tomorrow. What time is it now? Almost eight o'clock. See what you can do at your end, Ashenden. Inquire in Windsor, Richmond. You never know. There may be someone around who's had experience cooking for a lumber camp. The man would have worked all winter, but he might be free now. You can never tell. It's a little late but I'm going to make some inquiries right now. It's short notice. It's also an emergency. We'll pay double wages if we have to."

"That's a good incentive, sir. Still, we have to find the right person first. And a crew for him."

"Andosca had all four of his sons working with him, didn't he?"

"He did, sir, but only three of them were on the payroll, and only two of them were working with him in the kitchen. The other was hired on as a labourer. Young Ralph Andosca was helping out in the kitchen now and again; as I mentioned, he also helped out elsewhere. If we can find the right man, he should be able to make do with two helpers just as Andosca did."

"See what you can find at your end, Ashenden, and I'll make inquiries here."

"One more thing, sir. Will we cover travel for the Andoscas?"

"Yes, of course. And put them in a Second Class carriage. Andosca's a good man; he deserves as much."

"Very well, sir."

"I'll be there tomorrow, Ashenden. I won't be able to make it in the morning but perhaps I can catch the afternoon train. No need to meet me. I'll get a horse from the livery stable."

"Very well, sir."

"Damn shame. I still can't believe it. The youngest one, too. Nice lad. What was his name?"

"Ralph, sir."

"Makes you wonder what the world is coming to."

"Indeed it does."

"I spoke too soon, today, Ashenden. Things were going too well. Should have known something would happen. Always does. Let's get on it then. Good night, Ashenden."

As the judge placed the earpiece back on its hook, the first thought that came to his mind was inconsequential and almost irreverent: by now, his coffee would be cold.

Chapter 7

Ashenden and the coroner disembarked from the wagon after the high constable, who all but leapt from his seat. They made a point of staying several paces back to allow the policeman all the room he needed to examine the scene of the murder. There was a dark, irregular stain on the beaten earth, but nothing that could lead an untrained eye to identify it as spilled blood. The stain might as easily have been the result of an accidental spill of coal oil, or creosote, or some other dark and viscous liquid.

Nevertheless, Moe studied the ground attentively for a few minutes, aware that the murder had occurred more than twelve hours earlier. At least half a dozen pairs of work boots had trampled around the stain. Moe could picture the event from what Ashenden had told him on the ride from the train station. He wasn't surprised that the ground could tell him nothing.

He stood and slowly scanned the surroundings. Back, from where they had come, the rail bed cut a long, level line that eventually fell from view into woodland. To his right and left the forest was dark, dense with undergrowth. Ahead the line ran straight and level before curving to the left and disappearing into the trees.

Moe found similarly little to see around the pile of debris that rose several yards from the rail bed, its encroaching bulk edging almost into the woods. Around the pile, the terrain was uneven, and littered with clods of earth, stones, wood chips, twigs, and branches. The mound itself rose to a height of seven or eight feet. It was an irregular pile of dirt, of rocks and stones and small boulders, of bark, branches, and splintered logs. It was one of dozens, rising at irregular intervals on both sides of the rail bed. Here and there around the mound, in places where the earth was soft or muddy, he could see the imprint of a toe, or heel, but nothing remotely helpful other than a single partial print that seemed to point towards the dense woods. Moe walked all the way around the pile but there was nothing to see. There was even less in the dense undergrowth where tracks would be impossible to follow. There was only the scantest evidence—a broken branch at waist height—that a fugitive might have fled through the woods.

"Not much to see here, is there?" Moe was speaking more to himself than to Ashenden. As they returned to the wagon he asked, "Will the boy who witnessed the shooting be at the camp? I want to speak to him first."

"He's there waiting for us," Ashenden assured him. Richard Todd had arrived at the camp just after seven, as he had been doing three or four days a week for much of the summer. Ashenden had made a point of seeing him, but the boy looked fine, and showed no outward signs of the shock he had experienced the evening before.

From a distance, there was no sign at the camp that the previous day's tragedy had occurred. The few men to be seen in the large clearing seemed to be going about their business with purposeful strides. The site was calm and quiet. Sunlight seemed to play with the plume of blue smoke that rose almost straight up from the cook tent, wavering only slightly in the all-but-imperceptible breeze. Faint but unidentifiable cooking smells reached them, surprisingly far from the tent itself, as did the muffled sounds that escaped from the same place. It was only Ashenden who was aware of a grey tarpaulin hiding something in the shade of the trees at the eastern edge of the clearing.

Ashenden steered the team in that direction. He removed the tarp to reveal a coffin of rough lumber. Ashenden removed the coffin's lid and Moe glanced quickly at the body of Ralph Andosca. The boy's arms had been crossed over his chest.

"We'll have to turn him over," said the coroner, "just for a minute."

Ashenden took the boy's shoulders, Moe his feet, and as they lifted turned the body to reveal a large, ugly, brown stain surrounding a tattered and pockmarked patch of cloth and flesh.

"You can put him back as he was," said the coroner. "Cause of death is pretty clear. You can take the body. I'll need just a few minutes to draw up a death certificate. I don't want to put you to any trouble but if I could get a ride back to the train station to catch the 11:00 southbound, I would appreciate it."

"Of course," Ashenden assured the doctor. "We have trestle tables you can use, there, in the big tent. I'll find a man who can drive you to the station, and, if you don't mind, I'd send the body to the undertaker's at the same time. I'll be near the cook tent, Doctor, when you're done."

Ashenden and Moe spotted Richard Todd by a woodpile, splitting wood that he was then stacking near the cook tent entrance. As they approached, Frank Andosca, middle-aged and heavy-set, wearing a vast white apron, stepped out of the cook tent.

"Oh, Andosca! This is High Constable Moe."

Roderick Moe had his own opinions, but he was on duty, where he was a professional. Moe was a relatively young man who had joined the force only after trying his hand at a few other jobs. He had gone back to school to obtain his matriculation, and he'd joined the police with the ambition to be a captain when he retired.

"I'm sorry for your loss," were Moe's first words but he did not hold out his hand.

Andosca looked at the policeman with eyes that seemed not to see anything. "You catch him first, 'cause me, I kill him with bare hands," Andosca's face contorted to control his tears.

Moe ignored the cook's words. With calmness he didn't feel, he replied, "I have to ask you a few questions. I'll come back, right after I speak to the lad, over there."

As Andosca turned to go back to his stoves, Ashenden stepped forward and put his hand on the cook's arm. "*Aspetta un minuto, Andosca,* the coroner is writing up the death certificate. He'll release Ralph's body as soon as he's done. I've made arrangement with the undertaker, and I've got the train schedules, if you want to look at them with me..."

"Inna minute. I gotta go look kitchen first," Andosca replied. "I be back."

"Todd! This is High Constable Moe. He has to ask you some questions."

"Give me your full name, lad, and tell me what happened yesterday afternoon."

Moe listened attentively, his notepad in one hand and pencil in the other, as the boy recounted again the events of the previous evening. Richard Todd was surprised to realize that those events were already losing the crystal clarity they had had the evening before when he told his parents, and sisters, why he was back so late.

"Can you describe the man?" Moe asked.

"I only saw him for just a second," the boy replied. "There was something about him...I don't know. It was all so fast. When I saw him, he was already stepping towards the woods. He disappeared almost right away behind the pile of stones and stuff and he was gone."

"Can you tell me anything about him? Was he tall? Short? What did he look like?"

"I didn't see him really. He was sideways like. And he was bent over and running crouched, and he moved real fast, so I didn't get a real look at him. I didn't get to see his face or nothing like that."

"Can you tell me how he was dressed?"

"I don't know. Just ordinary clothes. He wasn't wearing no special clothes or nothing."

"Was he dressed like a workman, like one of the construction crew?"

"No, not really. Everyone here's all dressed in blue coveralls, like. He wasn't dressed in blue coveralls. His pants was dark, I think, and his shirt was a lighter colour, not white or nothing, but lighter, like a tan colour."

"Was he wearing a hat?"

"Yes, he was. It was dark, maybe green or brown. I couldn't really say the colour, but it was dark. It was sort of crumpled, as if it was an old hat."

"Did he seem young or old?"

"I don't know. He couldn't have been that old 'cause he moved pretty fast. I didn't really see him for more than a second, I don't think."

"And he had a gun?"

"A long gun. I couldn't tell what kind but from the sound I knowed it was a shotgun, and when I saw Ralph, I knowed that's what it was."

"If you saw him again, do you think you'd recognize him?"

"I don't know. There was something about him, but I don't know. I didn't really see him. Though I suppose if I saw him again and he was wearing the same clothes and I saw him run off to the right, I might be able to say if it was him."

"Do you work here as part of the construction crew?"

"Sometimes, if my dad don't need me at home, I might haul sand or gravel with our wagon, usually it's three or four days a week. Like today, I brought the wagon up but I gotta get back home to help my dad. I was just chopping a bit of wood while I was waiting 'cause that's what Ralph always did."

Moe found Frank Andosca far more difficult to interview than young Richard Todd, but he had expected that would be the case. Still, even when Andosca got upset, Moe stayed calm, professional.

"What you ask me? Why? Why you not find man who kill my son?"

He had explained, "I have to start with you, Mr. Andosca, because you can tell me more about Ralph than anyone else. The more I know about Ralph, the better my chances are of discovering why he was killed, and that should lead us to who killed him. I only have a few questions. It won't take long."

Roderick Moe conducted the interview by the book. His report would be faultless, and as comprehensive as the few scant facts he had so far gleaned might allow. He hadn't liked the sound of it last night when he'd taken the telephone call, and he liked it less and less as he went along. He hadn't jumped to any conclusion, but he had hoped that the murder was some sort of twisted revenge, a young boy murdered to exact vengeance on the father. That would have meant the killer was someone known to the father, hence one of the labourers. This possibility had now grown very faint, but Moe wasn't at all sure where else a motive might be lurking.

As he answered Moe's questions, something slowly swept over Frank Andosca. He seemed visibly to shrink, as if he'd been a balloon deflating through a slow leak. By the end, he was speaking to the floor, in a lifeless monotone.

"Enemies? Wit his brothers, he fight alla time, but is boys, so they fight alla time. But not enemies. No. And me? I have enemies you tink I know who dey are? You, you know your enemy, you tink? Me, I mine my own business. I don't make no enemies. But, dis I tell you. I got one enemy. De man who kill my son."

Chapter 8

There were far too many men for Moe to try to interview individually, especially since he knew the interviews would reveal nothing. Moe settled on another plan. It was safe to assume that the killer had acted alone; after all, Richard Todd had described a single individual who had taken a single shot. Moe asked Ashenden to assemble the men before their meal. He then asked that the men group themselves into the same work crews of which they were a part at the end of the afternoon, when the murder occurred. He went from one set of men to another.

"I want you all to think back to late yesterday afternoon, between 5:30 and 6:30," he told the men. "I want you to look at the others in your group and tell me if all those men were with you during that time. Point to anyone who wasn't with you, who left your work crew between 5:30 and 6:30."

The response was what he had expected.

"Thank you," he said to Ashenden, "they can go."

"I'm glad it wasn't any of my men."

"No, I don't think it can be. They were all accounted for at the time of the shooting. Besides, there's the problem of the shotgun, which I think is a .410. You've told me that you've got two firearms here on site, a long gun and a pistol."

"Locked in my armoire, as you saw."

"And neither of them could have been the murder weapon. Neither of them has been fired recently. From what you tell me, there's no motive among your men either, there's no one who has it in for the father. You say he's well liked."

"They like his food, so they like him. Andosca doesn't mix all that much with the others. Not because he's unpleasant or antisocial, but they're all labourers, and he's the cook. They don't ever rub elbows on the job, and we work pretty much from sunrise to sunset. So, aside from the minute it takes him to dole out mashed potatoes onto a man's plate, he doesn't really see much of the other men. There's not much socializing after dark."

"There's a train at 2:00 that I want to catch back to Sherbrooke. Before I leave, I wonder if I can get you to confirm a few things for me."

"Anything at all."

"Andosca says he's from Albany, in New York. Is that correct?"

"As far as I know, yes. He has a home in a small town called Troy, just outside of Albany."

"How did he happen to come to work here? He's originally Italian, but he's now an American, is that correct? Why is he working here in Canada, in the Eastern Townships?"

"It was Judge Foster who hired him, along with the entire crew at the same time. Judge Foster has connections in Albany, connections with railway people. These are all men, or almost all, who have experience building railways. They've worked, almost all of them, all over half of eastern North America. Andosca is part of the crew. Their winter break, depending where they're working, can be anywhere from two to five months, and Andosca spends it at his home in Troy. Most of the crew are from the same area.

"As far as I know, he has a wife and six children; one girl and five boys. The girl and the youngest boy are at home with their mother. The oldest boy, Sheldon, works as a labourer, on full pay. The two other boys, Tyler and Drake, work with him in

59

the kitchen as his scullery boys. The youngest of the boys here, Ralph, wasn't an employee. He wasn't on the payroll. I made a point every payday of giving him a dollar or two, but he was only here because he was his father's son. But he was a helpful lad. Andosca generally had some job near the cook tent for him to do. Ralph was never a problem. He was generally around the kitchen, although it happened that he might help out here and there whenever someone called him to help with something that needed an extra pair of hands and that Ralph could do. He loved horses, and that was the only reason he was riding back with the Todd boy. The fact is, the horse that Ralph was riding could as easily have been tied to the wagon. It was Ralph who wanted to ride him back to the Todd farm. It's something he had done any number of times."

"Have you had any strangers hanging about?"

"No. The first mile of subgrade we laid was close to the village, so we had people sometimes watching from a distance, but now we're well out of town and cutting through bush, so the answer to your question is no. No one has cause to come out here, except for the Catholic priest from Windsor, Father Thomas Quinn. We've arranged to have him come out every second Sunday to celebrate mass—weather permitting, of course; when it's pouring rain, as it was last Sunday, he doesn't come."

"So there's no contact between your crew and the townspeople, is that right?"

"It's minimal. We keep the work crew on OMR property at all times. If something's needed in town, I'm generally the one who goes. Otherwise, the only other person who goes in regularly is Tyler Andosca. Three days a week, Mondays, Wednesdays and Fridays he takes the light wagon to the Express Office to pick up his father's order. As far as I know, the only people he'd have dealings with would be at the train station, and I've never heard of a problem of any kind. He's also been to the blacksmith's a few times. Conrad Beaulieu is the man's name. His shop is a little further up, maybe an eighth of a mile past the train station. He's on Main Street so you can't miss him. But I've had no report of any kind of a problem from him either. I occasionally send Tyler there to bring in or pick up something that needs repair or replacing, since he's going into town in any case. He's also been to the hardware store once or twice, but again, I haven't heard of any kind of problem with Tyler there either."

"Thank you, Mr. Ashenden. I think I've learned as much as I can here, even if there wasn't much to learn. What time is it? I should have time to make my train, unless the station master has a lot to say."

"If he does, I hope it helps find the murderer. I'd be glad to see the man caught. It's a terrible thing. Ralph was a clever lad, a lovely boy. I'd like to see whoever did it caught and hanged."

"If he is caught, he certainly will hang. And I will do my best to catch him."

"I'll have the light wagon hitched immediately and one of the men will drive you back to the train station. Good luck," said Ashenden, extending his hand to the high constable.

Chapter 9

It was inevitable that the murder of young Robert Audette in Farnham earlier in the week would be on Roderick Moe's mind as he made his way back to the Windsor train station. When he had set out early that morning for the murder site on the OMR, he wondered if there might be some link between the two killings, perhaps even the work of the same criminal. What if the two murders—both of which had for a victim a young male who was a railroad employee—had been committed towards a common end, or by the same perpetrator?

Now, returning from the OMR site, it was clear that despite those coincidences, the two murders had not been carried out by the same hand. The Audette murder had been a vicious, perhaps even sadistic, act. The Andosca murder had been as quick as it was brutally efficient.

Moe wondered if this was what was called a contract killing. He had no personal experience with gangland hit men, although he'd certainly read a number of stories about the Italian Mafia and the Cosa Nostra, and given that Andosca was Italian, this was where his thoughts now ran. Nothing he'd seen or heard pointed towards one of the OMR's Italians committing the crime, but he wondered if someone else in Andosca's past might not have wanted to exact revenge on the camp cook by killing his young son. Had Andosca run afoul of the Mafia? It was a possibility he would have to look into, and he made a mental note to contact his law enforcement counterparts in Troy, New York, to see what they could tell him about Andosca.

The shooting was a mystery and Moe acknowledged that, much as he would like to catch the murderer, in his heart, he was in no way confident that he would manage to do so. Nevertheless, he would speak to the station master to see if there was anything to learn even if, according to Ashenden, neither Andosca nor any of the Italians (save one) had any dealings with the good citizens of Windsor.

Still, if there was a silver lining it was that the victim was a foreigner, and an Italian at that. In the case of Audette, it was a local lad who had been killed. The murder, very brutal murder, of young Audette no doubt would have the lad's family and friends pressuring the police for an arrest; all of Farnham would be clamoring for swift justice for the perpetrator. It was one of their own who'd been killed, and not just anyone, but the son of an important town functionary. The pressure on the investigating officer would be enormous.

Moe realized that it was lucky for him that Ralph Andosca was a stranger. No doubt, all of Windsor, all of the Eastern Townships for that matter, found the murder shocking, but no one was personally touched by it. No one had lost a family member or a close friend. It wasn't even a Canadian who had been killed. Ralph Andosca was just an Italian, or rather an Italian American, if the distinction was relevant.

Roderick Moe thought again of the way he'd handled the interview with Andosca, and he felt proud of how professionally he had conducted it.

In Windsor, Moe began at the train station.

The station master was a middle-aged man by the name of Fortier who spoke English almost perfectly. Fortier confirmed that a young Italian came to the Express Office three times a week to pick up a wagonload of goods shipped in from Montreal. He had learned the young Italian's name only recently but had never had any direct dealings with him, never spoken with him. He knew that the young man always sent a telegram when he came in, and he always arrived about fifteen minutes before the Southbound 3:47. He knew that once the telegram was sent, he'd line up and wait with his wagon along the Express Office loading ramp. The goods were always foodstuffs and always came from Montreal. The young man always helped with the loading of his wagon, which wasn't always the case for all the customers at the Express Office, Fortier wanted to point out. There had never been any problems with the young Italian of any kind, that he was aware of. No, no money problems at all; money had never exchanged hands because once a month Mr. Percy came in to settle the OMR's bill, and they'd never had any late payment problems with the Orford Mountain Railway. As with everyone else, Fortier was shocked by the killing and hoped that the murderer would soon be caught and hanged from the gallows.

The chief constable thanked the station master, checked his watch, confirmed the time of the next train, and set off at a brisk pace to speak to Conrad Beaulieu.

The blacksmith was a young man, tall and wiry, and with a head of wavy red hair. His English was broken but understandable, and in fewer than five minutes the chief constable was walking, at a less hurried pace, back to the train station, his on-site enquiries completed.

It did cross his mind that, having unlimited time, he might interview the occupants of the several dozen houses and establishments between the Greenlay bridge and the point at which Tyler Andosca left the River Road to access the rail bed of the OMR, but to what avail? At most, a few of them might have noticed Tyler Andosca driving his wagon to or from the station, and how could that possibly help his investigation? And if Tyler Andosca had stopped—or even if he were in the habit of stopping regularly at the spring that the high constable had noticed on the River Road—what significance could there be to that?

No, the high constable decided, he would catch the train to Sherbrooke. There were other issues waiting for him at the station that promised far more satisfactory conclusions. And who could say? With a little time, perhaps something, or someone, might appear out of thin air to shed some light on the death of the boy.

As it turned out, Moe received a tip, in the form of an anonymous letter, about two men, strangers to the area, who seemed to be living in a makeshift cabin off the River Road, not that far from the new OMR rail spur.

Very early on the morning of August 23, High Constable Moe, acting on the tip from a good citizen of Melbourne Township, and accompanied by three of his men, descended on a small makeshift shack at the end of a long trail that led into the woods from the west-bank River Road.

When he barged in through the door (which was neither locked nor barred) he startled the two men, who were only half-dressed and who were sitting on upturned boxes at a rickety table smoking cigarettes and drinking coffee.

He promptly arrested them, informed them they were being charged with murder, handcuffed them, and walked them back along the narrow path to a waiting wagon.

Omer Ayette and Georges St. Pierre were new to the area. The land they were on was Crown land. The cordwood they were cutting—a meagre two and a half runs of mixed hardwood near their shack—suggested that they were not very hard workers, or that they were only pretending to be woodcutters to hide their criminal activities. They had a shotgun, supposedly to shoot rabbits and partridges which they claimed to be their main food source. There was also a red kerchief found in the cabin, such as that worn by the men who had attempted to rob Percy a month earlier. Red, unfortunately, was a popular colour for kerchiefs and other apparel that summer so the item itself was far from uncommon; still, for High Constable Moe it had the potential of being a convincing piece of evidence.

It was put to Ayette and St. Pierre that their motive for killing young Andosca was robbery, and that they were really after Richard Todd who had eighty dollars in his pockets.

Even though the two men proclaimed their innocence, they were promptly incarcerated in the large, intimidating, recently built jail on Winter Street in Sherbrooke.

On two occasions they were hauled out of their cells and made to sit for a time in a small, windowless, brightly lit room which had a relatively large mirror hung on one wall. The first time it was Charles Percy and his son who stared at them intently from the other side of the one-way mirror. The second time it was Richard Todd.

Percy couldn't say if these were the two who had sprung out of the woods to steal the payroll. Even when Ayette and St. Pierre tied red kerchiefs over the bottom half of their faces, Charles Percy couldn't say. They might have been—especially with the kerchiefs on—but they could just as easily not have been the would-be robbers. If there had been a single thing that he could identify in them, he would have gladly played his part in seeing them incarcerated for as long as possible. But Percy didn't want to send innocent men to jail, and these two looked innocent—at least of the attempted robbery.

Richard Todd wanted to please the police. He wanted to see Ralph's murderer hung on the gallows. But it was confusing. One at a time, he had to look at the two men and pick the one whose silhouette had stepped so quickly off the rail bed and into the woods. Was it the larger man or was it the smaller? It was late afternoon, meaning that when he looked back over his shoulder, he was looking west, towards the sun which was not yet setting but definitely lower in the sky. It was so difficult, seeing these two men sitting in a bare room, to make of either one the murderer who dashed so quickly into the woods.

A few days later High Constable Moe received the results of tests carried out in Montreal. The shotgun he had confiscated from the two men had been ruled out as the weapon that had killed Ralph Andosca.

Ayette and St. Pierre had lost three weeks during which they might have been cutting and splitting cordwood. On the other hand, they both left the Winter Street jail a pound or two heavier than when they had been brought in.

The mistaken arrest was as close as Moe got to solving the murder, or the robbery. The inquiries he'd made of his American counterparts in Troy turned up a blank. Andosca was not known to them, and had never crossed their path. There was nothing else for Moe to go on, and the case was quietly put on the back burner.

Similarly, the story faded from the press. In all, the *Sherbrooke Daily Record* ran a total of four stories on the murder, each briefer than the one before, and each buried a little deeper in the paper. In the days immediately after the killing, the story had been reported relatively far afield, as sensational stories are wont to do. Among other papers to report the murder was the *Knickerbocker News*, which served the Albany area. It sent a reporter to Ralph Andosca's funeral, which was held on the Saturday following his murder, and which gave the paper occasion to repeat the original, and sensational, story.

For people who keep track of such things, the incomprehensible nature of the murder on the Orford Mountain Railway was just one more of life's mysteries.

Chapter 10

A mystery a little bit like our screen, I see. Shawn needs a few more minutes.

Since I can't show you anything for the moment, let me tell you a little about Judge Samuel Foster and the Orford Mountain Railway. It was, after all, on OMR property that Ralph Andosca was murdered, and it was because of Judge Samuel Foster that Ralph was there, in August of 1905, in all innocence, to be murdered.

Samuel Willard Foster was born in 1827 in Frost Village, which, in spite of its name, is not really more than a hamlet; and he died in 1915, in Knowlton, only fifteen kilometers from where he was born. About halfway between the place where he was born and the place where he died is the hamlet of Foster, named in his honour. Appropriately enough, railway tracks still run through Foster.

Judge Foster was an important and influential man, and well-known in his day. Albeit, not as well-known as his famous—or perhaps it would be better to say infamous—older brother, Asa Belknap Foster who helped give the term "railway tycoon" a very pejorative connotation, roughly synonymous with unscrupulous con man.

Ten years older than Samuel, Asa left home at the age of twenty to join his uncle in business. S. K. Belknap was an ambitious American railroad contractor, and Asa spent fifteen years working for and with him before returning to Canada in 1852 and settling in Waterloo, Quebec, just two or three miles from Frost Village where he had grown up and gone to school. A hint of the wealth that Asa Foster amassed before turning forty is the thirty-room mansion he built for his wife and ten children, a stately and sumptuous structure that is now a boutique hotel with an upscale restaurant.

In Canada, Asa Foster picked up where he had left off in the New England States. He got involved with commerce and banking, as well as with railways. He also got involved in politics, as his father had before him. In the colonial years prior to Confederation he was a follower of George-Étienne Cartier, and when the Dominion of Canada was created in 1867, Asa Foster was named to the Senate.

However, things soured for him. He found himself embroiled in a scandal that brought down the Conservative government of John A. Macdonald, and in 1877, a decade after Confederation, Asa Foster died bankrupt and dishonoured. He is accredited with a witticism that further tarnished his star: what's the point of having friends if you can't use them?

Samuel Foster trod a much straighter and narrower path than his older brother. Samuel was the fifth and youngest son of a medical doctor who, in 1822, moved his family from Vermont to Lower Canada. Dr. Foster was following the lead of thousands of other New Englanders who, in the first few decades of the nineteenth century, opted to exchange the freedom promised by a newly-minted republic for the potential of richer, more arable acreage in a British colony that was anxiously seeking immigrants and luring them with the promise of land that could be inexpensively had.

The Fosters were a well-to-do family, not because Samuel's father was a doctor, a profession far less lucrative in those days than it is today, but because his mother was a Belknap, born into a wealthy New England railroad family. Like his older siblings, Samuel was educated in a one-room schoolhouse in Frost Village, although his upbringing was less modest than this might imply. The Foster boys often spent holiday time with their Belknap cousins in Vermont. Samuel, as an adolescent, had the opportunity to visit cities like Boston and New York. Deprivation was not part of the family vocabulary.

When he left school, he found work as a clerk in the law office of Everett Baylor in nearby Knowlton. A few years later, before the age of twenty-one, he took his bar exam and joined Baylor in practice. Several years later, Samuel married Evangeline Richardson who was four years his senior, a doctor's widow with two children. The family lived in the house on the Lakeshore Road that Doctor Richardson had bequeathed to his widow. Samuel fathered two children with Evangeline, two girls, some of whose fifth and sixth generation descendants still live in the area.

Foster did well at law, in both senses of the word. He had a good legal mind, but he also had a good deal of common sense. He won more cases than he lost, but more important, many of his cases did not go to court at all. He was often able to negotiate settlements that were not necessarily fully satisfactory to either party, but were nonetheless grudgingly acceptable to both, and had the financial benefit of avoiding court costs. His clients rarely begrudged the legal fees he charged, even if another lawyer might perhaps have charged a little less for the same work.

Foster did well at law and at least as well as a landlord. Like his brothers, he had been given some advantages at birth, but to his credit, he had squandered very little, if any at all, of the capital he had been given. Rather, he had invested wisely. From the time he took his bar exam he had started acquiring property. He bought houses and rooming houses in places like

Waterloo and Magog, but also farms as far afield as St. Mary's and Deauville. He bought his properties shrewdly and kept an eye on their management. The rents he collected provided a stream of additional income. His rents were a supplement to the fees he collected as a lawyer, but later, as his holdings grew, they provided a very comfortable, independent income.

In 1872, five years after Confederation, when he was forty-five, Samuel Foster was appointed Judge of the Quebec Court in Knowlton's not-yet-built courthouse.

The same year, the family moved from the home on Lakeshore Road where Samuel and Evangeline had lived since being married to a newly built house that was only modest by comparison to Asa's mansion in Waterloo. The new Foster home was a stately stone structure with seventeen rooms. It was set on four acres of partially wooded land that had frontage on Victoria Street and ran back to the shores of Brome Lake.

In what became an annual tradition, the Judge and Evangeline hosted a picnic for the citizens of Knowlton and the surrounding villages on the second Sunday in July, and then in February hosted a similar skating party. These continued until the turn of the century when Evangeline passed away and Samuel was over seventy. The raison d'être of the original fête had been to celebrate the judgeship and the new courthouse.

Judge Foster was quite young when he was appointed to the bench, and he was correspondingly young when he stepped down from the bench at the age of fifty-seven in 1884.

Four years later he was the general manager and principal shareholder of the newly chartered Orford Mountain Railway. There is a lot of room for speculation as to why Foster, who was sixty-one in 1888 when the OMR obtained its charter, would have embarked on such an enterprise. There were certainly reasons for Foster not to undertake such an endeavour, not the least of which was the example of his older brother.

The first railway in Canada had been built in 1836 when Samuel wasn't yet ten years old. It had been built by John Molson to run freight between the St. Lawrence River and Lake Champlain so as to facilitate shipping between Montreal and New York. Its example had been followed by a railroad in Nova Scotia, also hauling freight, and then another. Around the middle of the century, the colonial government began actively encouraging the construction of railroads as a means to further exploit the timber and mineral wealth of the colony. For the next decade and longer, there was an unprecedented construction boom throughout Lower and Upper Canada that saw the creation of a new aristocracy, the railroad barons.

Of course, as Samuel Foster had seen from up close, fortunes were also lost on railway ventures. Asa Foster had been far from the first, and would not be the last, to lose everything between two parallel rails of hot-rolled steel. It would be an exaggeration to say that there were as many railway bankruptcies as there were railways, but the truth was not far off. The investment required to lay down a rail line was enormous, and the return on that investment was often uncertain.

Yet there were other factors that led Samuel Foster to build a railroad. One, arguably, was that he had a bit of the railroader in his blood. His maternal uncle in New England had been a builder of railroads, as had his brother Asa, and Samuel would appear to have been genetically predisposed to follow their footsteps. Another factor may have been a desire to somehow atone for Asa's sad end. If Samuel could succeed where Asa had failed, he might perhaps redeem the Foster name on History's ledger sheet.

Had this been today, it's possible that, given Judge Foster's considerable wealth, the Orford Mountain Railway might have been construed as a retirement project.

For Samuel Foster, these emotional explanations likely would have been but secondary influences. It's more likely that

Foster saw in the OMR a genuine building block, an admittedly small railway by continental standards, but one that would play a significant initial role, and then, in the intermediate term, would play a different but no less useful one.

In a first phase, the OMR would be in a position to transport principally timber, but also other raw products such as slate, from Melbourne Ridge and Kingsbury, to a primary line, the Canadian Pacific Railway that ran through Eastman. Foster had no way of knowing, or possibly even of estimating, when these natural resources might give out, but he knew that eventually they would. However, in a second phase, he wanted to push the OMR beyond Kingsbury and right to the St. Francis River where it would be able to connect with the Grand Trunk Railway, and thus be able to serve as a conduit to connect Canada's two major lines.

Foster began construction of the OMR in 1891 and by 1894 the railway was operating from Kingsbury to Eastman, and doing so profitably, even if those profits were relatively modest. Then, just after the turn of the century, Foster decided to undertake the construction of an extension of this line to run from Kingsbury to Greenlay, across the St. Francis River from Windsor. With this extension the OMR would have one terminus in Eastman where the Canadian Pacific Railway had a station, and the other terminus just across the river from a Grand Trunk Railway station in Windsor. Passengers and merchandise would, with very little effort, be able to get from one major rail line to the next.

Chapter 11

Following a lifetime of enriching habits, Judge Foster kept a watchful eye on his railroad project. He quite regularly made the trek from his comfortable home in Knowlton out to the backwoods of Melbourne Township to follow the progress of his construction crews. As with any ambitious enterprise there were always at least a few problems; small ones when things were going well, big ones when they weren't.

We can imagine that on Tuesday, August 15, the judge left home a little after seven, under unpromising grey skies. Monday, it had rained intermittently much of the day and he feared that Tuesday could be a continuation of the same. Had it not been for an engagement later in the week, and had he not been prevented from visiting the worksite the week before, he might have delayed his visit further. But he had multiple reasons to make the trip, and so he set off with his small valise, despite the grey skies.

The weather to some extent mirrored the judge's mood which had been affected by the previous day's news of the murder of young Audette in Farnham, only thirty-five miles away. The murder had been as shocking for the judge as for anyone else, if not more so. Among his employees were call boys like Audette and the judge couldn't help questioning whether the murder was in some way linked to the boy's role as a railway employee. If that were the case, were there steps he could take to ensure the safety of his own call boys? Everything about the murder was a mystery and it had left him unsettled, like the weather.

Happily, during the ride to Bolton, the sky started turning a lighter shade of grey and even began to show promising hints of blue. The judge sat comfortably in the back seat of his Fossmobile, a vehicle he had acquired two years before while Provencher, who was his mechanic and his chauffeur, as well as his general handyman, drove. The car made good time, the road having proven to be in better condition with fewer ruts and puddles than might have been expected, and he arrived in Bolton a good ten minutes earlier than he had anticipated.

Bolton was a flag stop on the northbound run, and he was pleased to see that the flag was up and that there were a few people already waiting on the platform; several others joined them before eight-twenty-nine when Engine 4 coasted into the station exactly on time.

He was pleased to see that the passenger carriage was about a third full. It was freight traffic that kept the Orford Mountain Railway in the black, and any passenger traffic was, from an economic point of view, almost as much a public service as a source of income. However, an extra cipher on the credit side of the ledger was never unwelcome.

Samuel Foster had read recently that a mail train in England, running from Plymouth to London, had recorded a speed of one hundred miles per hour, achieving this over a measured quarter mile of track. The quarter mile was undoubtedly a stretch of track in excellent repair, and a mail train would be as light as a train could be: the engine, a 4—4—0, had been pulling only its tender and a single car, and a light one at that; mail cars carried far less weight than freight cars or half-full passenger carriages. Still, the thought of one hundred miles per hour rather made his head spin. Any sort of comparison to his own rail line was impossible. The south of England, from the coast to the capital, is flat land with few grades, and those rather gentle. The Orford Mountain Railway had been laid as flat and level as possible, but despite that, the line dropped a full quarter mile on its total length of seventy miles. Grades were inevitable, as were bends and curves to circumvent bogs and lakes and the shoulders of mountains. More significantly, the Orford Mountain Railway was in the business of hauling logs, lumber, cordwood, ore, charcoal, dry goods, and other manner of freight, as well as a certain number of travellers. When his trains averaged speeds of thirty-eight miles per hour, the judge was more than pleased. It was not for the Orford Mountain Railway to hitch a single mail car to an engine and rush urgent intelligence from port to court.

As he watched the countryside fly by his window, the judge estimated that the engineer (he hadn't seen the man clearly, but thought it might be O'Shea—the judge prided himself on knowing the names of all his employees) was keeping a steady throttle at close to forty miles per hour, as he was supposed to. The line, here at its southern section, ran largely through forest. There was only one more flag stop before they pulled into Eastman, to add two gondola cars of ore from the short spur from a nearby copper mine.

At Eastman the engine had to take on more water and wood to make the run to Kingsbury. As well, a number of cars, including the two they had picked up at the copper spur, had to be uncoupled while others had to be added. The judge took advantage of the twenty-minute stop to look in briefly on the station. Things seemed quite in order and Davis, the new station master, had done a good job of sprucing up the waiting room since his last visit.

The train left Eastman on time. The stops at Lawrenceville, East Ely, and Flodden were no longer than the timetable indicated they would be. Some passengers disembarked while others came on board, and at times the passenger car was more than half-full, a rather good number of passengers for a weekday. According to the judge's timepiece, the train pulled into Kingsbury a full minute ahead of schedule.

Judge Foster left his carryall in Willard Taylor's office and walked with the station master the one hundred yards to the clearing on the bank of Salmon Creek. Here, despite its name, Salmon Creek was both wide and fast flowing. Upstream, Salmon Creek led languorously and sinuously through swamp and lowland to Lake Brompton; downstream it turned into spumes of white water rushing over rapids and small waterfalls downhill to the river valley. There it meandered its slow way to the St. Francis.

Over the low level rumble from the rapids not far below, it was possible to hear noises that an accustomed ear could identify as axe blades biting into wood, and now and again the crack of splintering timber followed by the dull thud of a tree trunk crashing to the ground. The men making those noises were invisible, hidden behind the dense curtain of forest on the east bank of the stream. Somewhere, just beyond the still new-looking stone and cement footing that stood solid and incongruous on the opposite shore, was a small gap in vegetation that marked the south end of the footpath left by surveyors that was, even now, being transformed into a railway track.

"That's music to my ears, Taylor."

"Yes, sir, I thought you'd be glad."

"And you say you first started hearing it on Monday?"

"Monday afternoon, sir, although it sounded faint-like. It was late afternoon and the air was heavy because the rain was coming in, whereas now, especially that the clouds have cleared and the sun's out, the air is light and sound carries. But even

77

taking all that into account, by the sound, I'd say those men are a good bit closer than they were just yesterday.

"Do you know how close they are to the river?"

"I couldn't say, sir. I'd just be guessing. If you wish, I could find a skiff and send a man across to walk down the trail a bit. He might have to walk a quarter mile or so, but I wouldn't think much more. The man couldn't get lost, the trail is well marked."

"I suppose we could do that, Taylor, but, no, never mind. I'll get a good idea from the other side tomorrow morning. Either way, I'd say they're close enough that we better start getting things ready over on this side."

The judge looked around. He was standing on a stone and cement abutment at the far edge of a clearing the size of a playing field. The land had been roughly levelled two years before and even though vegetation had started sprouting almost everywhere, nowhere was there anything more than tufts of knee-high grasses.

"I may have materials start being shipped as early as next week, Taylor. You'll get a telegram at least a day ahead of time. I'll leave it to you to find men and horses, two teams, at least. Get three if you can."

It was going to be heavy work. The men and horses would be hauling finished stone. Of this, there would be a relatively small amount, enough to finish the decorative stonework on the bridge footings so that they would be as smart as they were solid and sturdy. Most of the hauling would be steel, heavy metal beams that would form the truss bridge that would span the river. While the distance to be covered would be no more than the hundred yards between the railway station and the riverbank, the loading, and unloading of the construction materials would be heavy, backbreaking work, even with ropes, levers, and pulleys.

With Taylor half a step behind him, the judge made his way back to the station. He reclaimed his traveling bag, paid Taylor a compliment on the tidiness of his station, and climbed up on the small gig that was most often used by the Express Office but was now being commandeered to deliver him to the Brunswick Hotel in Richmond, with one short stop along the way.

As they made their way out of the village, he instructed the man to turn right onto the Salmon Creek Road rather than go straight to meet the Waterloo Road. The latter was a designated high road and at least nominally, in better condition. It ran north along the ridge towards Upper Melbourne and south towards Waterloo. But the judge preferred the Salmon Creek Road that ran approximately along-side the watercourse all the way down the valley.

Three years before, the judge had envisaged extending his railway spur alongside this very roadway. Indeed, he had made quite detailed plans to extend the Orford Mountain Railway by running it roughly parallel to the Salmon Creek Road down to the St. Francis and then veering north to Upper Melbourne where its terminus would be. This would have placed the OMR terminus across the river from Richmond, where OMR passengers and freight would have access to three destinations: the year-round harbour of Portland, Maine, on the Atlantic Ocean; Quebec City and shipping routes to the British Empire that spanned the globe; and Montreal and points west in a country that now covered the continent, all the way to Vancouver.

Despite a good deal of rather expensive lobbying, all of the judge's petitions proved fruitless. His proposal was denied. Somewhere, someone put a political spanner into the works. What the Judge conceived as a most beneficial project for all, someone else perceived as an economic threat. The judge had not yet puzzled out exactly who felt threatened and why.

On the other hand, when the Judge had presented the plans to run his rail line on the south side of Salmon Creek down to Golden Bay, and then turn upstream to establish a terminus in Greenlay, his idea had been given government approval almost immediately.

The judge shrugged his shoulders; it was water under the bridge and best forgotten.

The metaphor however was a reminder of sorts. It brought the Judge back to the present, to the construction project that was now underway, and that would soon entail the construction of a rail bridge to pass over the waters of Salmon Creek. He would have to have Ashenden dig out the blueprints—long since drawn up—and study them again in preparation.

When he looked up from his reverie the sky was turning that brilliant shade of cerulean blue that always lifted the judge's sprits a notch higher.

Chapter 12

The president of the Orford Mountain Railway was so lost in his thoughts that he almost forgot to have the driver stop at a small, inconsequential house tucked far back from the road on the St. Francis River flats. It was the spire of St. Andrew's Presbyterian Church suddenly coming into view that revived him from his very pleasant reveries, a happy consequence of having taken the Salmon Creek Road. Just past the church, at the bottom of the hill, he had the driver turn right into a long driveway.

"Find some shade for yourself and the horse," he told the driver nodding towards a tall, drooping willow, "I shan't be very long."

When the young artist opened the door to him, Judge Foster suspected that the young man had only just put down his brushes; how else to explain the shirt sleeves rolled up to the elbow and the unbuttoned collar?

"Have I come at a bad time?" inquired the judge.

"No, not at all. I was expecting you. I can show you the painting, if you wish. I was just touching up one or two little things, but it's pretty well finished."

"You work quickly." The judge intended his remark as a compliment, though after the words were out of his mouth, he hoped that they were taken as such.

"Please, come in through here."

The judge had been to the artist's studio once before to sit for him. As before he was struck by what seemed a disorganized if not chaotic workplace, although almost at once his eyes went to the relatively large canvas resting on an easel near the centre of the room.

"Oh, my!" was the exclamation that passed his lips despite himself. The portrait startled him much as an unexpected mirror might have. The first glance had elicited a spontaneous response; now the judge slowly and attentively took in the canvas, going over it square inch by square inch. He was pleased by the likeness, very pleased.

This was a far better portrait than the one he had commissioned some ten years earlier from an American artist who had worked slowly, charged dearly, and delivered a portrait that he had started to dislike almost from the moment he had hung it. At that time, it had been his cousin who had encouraged him to have his portrait done by a man who was the toast of Boston. He had had to stay in Boston a full extra week because the artist had requested multiple sittings.

This painting was different. Looking at it was eerily like looking at a reflection. It was a very good likeness. He saw himself in three-quarter size gazing serenely from the canvas. It was remarkable, and the more he looked at it, the more remarkable it became. Perhaps most startling was that, as distant background, Coburn had painted a view of the lake. How perceptive of the young artist to have chosen that particular view, one that the judge had always especially liked, and one that, as far as he knew, the young artist had seen but once.

"It will need time to cure," Frederick Simpson Coburn was telling him. "About two or three weeks. I'm not sailing before the end of next month, and you'll be able to have it well before then."

It wasn't just that Coburn had captured his likeness, but he had also captured his very essence. Was it in the eyes? Or in the set of his features? Or perhaps something else altogether? How much are we swayed by minor details, the judge wondered? Was it significant, for example, that Coburn had worked in a view of the lake over his left shoulder? Or that beside his figure in the painting was a small table on which one could see a well-worn copy of the Civil Code and a set of several keys on a ring, while an old fixed-globe lantern hung only half perceptibly behind his elbow?

"That will be fine," the judge replied, his tone almost distracted. He couldn't draw his eyes away from the portrait. He didn't want to be rude, but the painting was exercising a mesmerising effect on him. It took a physical effort to turn away from it.

"Shall I look after the framing?" The question, the judge realized, had been asked twice.

"Yes, by all means, whatever you choose will be fine, I'm sure."

The judge smiled fondly at the young man, this remarkable young man who had so little about him to mark him as such. He was relatively tall, perhaps taller than he at first seemed. He was slim, with fine bones and delicate hands—the hands, clearly, of a painter. He wore a thin moustache that, the judge supposed, was intended to make him look a little older. He was soft-spoken and shy. He was soberly dressed. Really, aside from his hands, there was nothing about him that suggested the considerable talent he obviously had. He might almost have passed for an accountant, or a bookkeeper.

"It will add ten per cent to the price we discussed."

"That will be fine." He turned his head to look again at the portrait. "It's a very fine painting," he told the young artist, "I like it very much."

"Thank you, sir."

"I should be thanking you. I must be off now. I have a man waiting. Good day, Mr. Coburn."

The decision to have his portrait done was made rather quickly but not without consideration. He had heard of this young painter only a few months previous when he had been a guest of Harold Crawdon in Waterville and seen a lovely portrait of Winona. The image of the painting remained clear in his mind, and the more he reflected on it, the more he thought of contacting Coburn himself.

Samuel Foster was not a vain man as, for example, his older brother, Asa, had been. He did not need a portrait of himself to satisfy his vanity. Yet, it would be false modesty to pretend that he had not contributed in a rather significant way to the greater community. His work had not been that of the subsistence farmer who ekes out of the land little more than what is enough to feed and husband himself and his family. His work had always been of a different kind, as had the accompanying remuneration that he had drawn. Yet the wealth he'd accumulated had never been—as it had for Asa—a grail unto itself. The money, of itself, had never been especially important, perhaps because it had always been there. The judge acknowledged that he lived well, but, he would have insisted, not lavishly or luxuriously. As well, he had always been, if not generous, at least giving. St. Paul's Anglican Church and its good works, for example, had been supported in a substantial way through his tithing. In myriad ways he had contributed to the easing of the frictions that came with the trade and exchange of commercial life, and sometimes with the vicissitudes of personal life as well. His enterprises—including and perhaps especially the Orford Mountain Railway—had contributed, and continued to contribute, to the public good; to add to the shared wealth of the greater community.

Samuel Foster was of an age that he had had time enough to consider his mortality, and what might be his legacy. Adding a portrait of himself to the goods and chattel he would be leaving behind to posterity was not, in his mind, an act of vanity but rather a small reminder. He imagined a distant descendant, a great-great grandchild years down the road, looking up and asking, "Who was that?" and being told something along the lines of, "That was your great-great-grandfather Foster; he was a footnote in history."

Besides, he had already had his portrait done. This was simply an upgrade, an improvement, a necessary amelioration. As soon as it arrived, he would hang it, and then take pleasure in burning the abomination that was hanging in the hall now. It pleased the judge that, at that moment, he couldn't remember even the name of the pretentious bohemian Boston fop who had done nothing more than waste an otherwise perfectly good piece of canvas.

It was but a short drive to Lower Melbourne and then across the new toll bridge and down Main Street to the Brunswick Hotel, directly across the street from the Grand Trunk Railway station. The hotel was a rather imposing brick building that still felt new. The judge took a room and then went down to the dining hall which enjoyed a good reputation for its fare. He was not disappointed, finding his meal as copious as it was enjoyable.

Judge Foster permitted himself a short rest before making his way to the livery stable where he rented a small buggy that he drove back to Upper Melbourne to a large plot of land that fronted on the River Road. This was land he had bought a few years earlier when his plan was to extend the OMR to Upper Melbourne rather than Greenlay. He was pleased to see that the two Marcotte brothers were already there. He hoped it augured well for the sale of the hundred and twenty acres.

Chapter 13

The judge had been an early riser all his life. He drew open the heavy curtains and glanced out his room's west-facing window that overlooked Main Street, the Richmond train station, the rail yards, and beyond those the river, the village of Lower Melbourne and the pastured hillsides now bathed in the light of a newly risen sun.

It was a glorious morning, full of promise. Had someone told Judge Foster that before the day was out he would be coping with the aftermath of the murder of a twelve-year-old boy on the new spur of the Orford Mountain Railway, he would have laughed in derision at such an impossibly ludicrous thought.

The judge took an early breakfast and was on board the Grand Trunk Railway's southbound train No. 8 that quit the Richmond station at exactly 7:03.

He had always found the now familiar run up to Windsor as pleasant as it was short. The GTR tracks ran upstream along the east bank of the river that here flowed rapidly, with few bends or twists and devoid of wide meandering loops. The river was almost always in view for the southbound passengers who sat on the starboard side of the coach car. This was the side on which the judge always sat. After they passed the wide, willow-lined mouth of Salmon Creek on the west bank, he searched for signs, few and subtle as they were from this distance, of the extension of the Orford Mountain Railway. In places the riverbank was dense with vegetation that swept upwards towards a ridge, in other places the valley floor was wider and tabletop flat; here and there the forest had been cleared for hayfields and pasturelands, for barns and farmhouses. Well beyond the fields and the forests that were in view, the judge knew, his railroad was being built. From Greenlay, on the valley floor, the tracks would run roughly parallel to the river as far as Golden Bay where they would veer inland and run uphill, skirting muskeg and slicing through hillocks, on a long, steady grade to the hills of Kingsbury. The two or three plumes of smoke he noticed rising above the skyline, he was quite certain, were markers of the progress being made.

Ashenden was waiting for him on the platform. "I trust you had a good trip, sir?"

"Very good trip, Ashenden, very good! Tell me, how close to Salmon Creek do you think the fellers might be?"

"Interesting you ask, sir..."

"Taylor brought me down to the riverbank yesterday and we could hear them. Still some distance, but near enough I should think."

"We are getting closer, sir, about a little less than a quarter mile I'd say. Despite the weather of the last few days, the lumber crews are advancing as much as three hundred yards a day. We're making good progress on all fronts."

They checked his bag and made their way to the street where they climbed onto a wagon and headed towards the Orford Mountain Railway's construction sites.

The survey papers indicated that it was twelve and a half miles from the Orford Mountain Railway's Kingsbury station to the new Greenlay terminus. As well as covering distance on a horizontal plane, the tracks also had to climb more than six hundred feet from Greenlay to their destination in Kingsbury; all of the vertical ascent in the last six miles. There, of course, as the judge had seen the day before, the new spur would have to span Salmon Creek to link to the present OMR terminus.

It took little time to reach the covered bridge that connected Windsor to Greenlay and noisily cross it to reach the west bank of the St. Francis. There they turned north on the River Road and half a mile further on turned away from the river and almost immediately came to a large clearing, two acres of beaten earth that would soon be the site of the rail yards and turning table of the Orford Mountain Railway. Ashenden turned the horse towards the north end of the clearing, in the direction of an opening from which Judge Foster could already envisage a locomotive spewing steam as it rolled majestically into the new Greenlay terminus.

The first thing that had pleased the judge was that, despite a generally rainy summer and in particular the rains of the last few days—today was the first time in four days that he had woken to a sunny morning—neither the packed earth in the future rail yard, nor the subgrade on the future rail bed leading out of Greenlay showed any signs of water damage: no pot holes, no washouts, not even any shallow puddles to speak of. The surface they were driving on was hardly even muddy. If the subgrade was holding up this well, the rail bed that was going to be laid on top of it would be equally well drained. Avoiding water damage was a cardinal consideration for the judge who wanted to lay down a rail line that would last like the roads he had once seen in Italy; roads that were still viable, still being used, that had been laid down by the Romans almost two thousand years before. The Italians were doing a good job, the judge reflected, because road construction was in their blood. They were, as someone had once told him, the builders of the world.

The gig moved along at a good clip. They saw not a single soul for the first three miles, although the construction crew had left plenty of signs of their presence. The relatively narrow, raised sub grade passed by a number of small clearings. A few of these, always on the side of the river and closer to Greenlay, were pastures or hay fields beyond which a barn, or a shed might be distantly glimpsed. Further along, the clearings appeared haphazardly at irregular intervals on either side of the sub grade and were unmistakeably corollaries of the construction of the rail spur. A couple of the clearings narrowed into roads that led almost immediately to sand beds and gravel beds that provided most of the raw materials needed in this first phase of construction. A few clearings had relatively large piles of twelve-foot logs of commercial value; these would eventually be loaded onto an OMR train and transported to a sawmill. Other clearings were marked by large, blackened circles where piles of branches had been set afire or areas where piles of debris had been heaped into mounds that looked as if they were the handiwork of giant insects.

At the spot where the attempted hold-up had occurred, they stopped for a minute, as they had the last time Judge Foster had visited.

"I suppose you've heard nothing more about it?" the judge inquired.

"Nothing, sir. I don't imagine we will hear anything. All in all, I think we were quite lucky. Percy might have been more seriously injured, or even killed for that matter. And I have to hand it to him for holding onto the payroll as he did. I wouldn't have thought the man had that kind of spirit."

"You're quite right, Ashenden, I think he surprised us all. Still, I'd like to catch the men behind it."

"As would I, sir, although I don't suppose we ever will. I'm inclined to think it was two young thugs who'd spent too much time in a tavern. I know the Italians were blamed, but that was impossible. For one thing, not a one of them has a firearm. Nor could any of them have disappeared from a work crew without it being noticed. It could not possibly have been one of our men."

"No, certainly not. I never thought for a minute that it could be."

"When you think about it, this was an odd spot to choose to lay an ambush. Had it been one of our men—if one of them were to want to commit such a crime—he would have been considerably more intelligent in selecting his ambush. My guess is two yobs who were too clever by half and they've long since run back to whatever badger hole they'd come out of. It wasn't one of our men, and, in my opinion, it wasn't anyone from the immediate area."

"I'm sure you're right, Ashenden. Either way, it won't happen again. Percy will have an armed guard with him when he arrives this afternoon. I'm a bit sorry that I won't be able to see it myself, but it should be quite a show. Soon enough Percy will be able to take the train to Kingsbury to pay the men."

The first crews they met were rolling the sub grade, compressing as much as possible the layers of sand and gravel that would later be topped with the rocks and stones—the ballast—on which the sleepers and rails would eventually be laid.

When they reached the camp, Judge Foster was pleased to see that it had been moved a full three miles farther along the line. Despite the work involved in moving the camp, it was sensible to have the men sleeping and eating as close as possible to where the majority of them were working. This camp, like the two others, had easy access to a respectable stream.

Streams were a mixed blessing. They necessitated the construction of culverts that would permit waterways to flow unimpeded along their accustomed course while supporting a rail bed solid enough for the hundreds of tons of rolling steel that had to cross them several times a day. There were a number of masons among the crew and Judge Foster was quite pleased with the arched culverts of stone and cement they had built so far. Yet, for all their inconvenience, streams were essential to the construction crew, not just for drinking water but also for cooking and cleaning. The judge noticed that here, as at the last camp, a length of hose had been jerry rigged to bring water to the two tents that housed the kitchen and the laundry. Foster and Ashenden abandoned the gig at the main camp and rode on horseback as far as possible before dismounting and finishing their inspection on foot.

Above the camp the future rail bed grew progressively rougher, from the stretch where sand and gravel were being laid to the stretch where tree trunks were being limbed and moved aside. In places, blasting was bringing the bedrock down to the required level. In other places rocks and gravel were being dumped to fill hollows up to level. In a few places, culverts were being installed. At the far end men with saws and axes were felling trees.

As Ashenden had hoped, Judge Foster was pleased.

"Tell your father that that was a fine meal," the judge told the adolescent boy who was picking up their plates and cutlery.

"Yes, sir. I'll tell him. Thank you, sir."

Ashenden and Foster had eaten *al fresco*, just outside of Ashenden's tent, on a small folding table in the shade cast by the awning that stretched out above the tent's entrance. There was just enough of a breeze that they'd not been bothered by mosquitoes or other flying insects. It had been a copious meal, and for the judge, singularly satisfying. In part this was because he'd had a very early breakfast and it was after one o'clock by the time they got back to the camp to eat, but also because the veal cutlets had been cooked to perfection and attractively served on a plate of potatoes and fresh vegetables.

Over lunch, Ashenden had assured him, "I always eat here by myself but it's always the same meal as the men. It's only when you make your visits that Andosca prepares something special. This kind of meal is just for you. Andosca feeds the men well, but not quite as well as this."

"Would the sirs like dessert with their coffee?" The young boy was again standing at their table, about to replace their near-empty pitcher of water with an almost full one that he now cradled in his arms.

"Desert as well?" exclaimed the judge. "That sounds quite tempting. Can you tell us what the dessert is?"

"Yes, sir. My father prepared a special cake for you, a *torta greca*. However, if you prefer you can have the peach cobbler that my brother has prepared for tonight's supper."

"Since your father prepared it especially for us, I'll take the cake. How about you, Ashenden?"

"Yes, I'll have that too."

"Two *torta greca* it is, then. Remind me of your name, young man."

"It's Ralph, sir."

"Tell me, Ralph, are you working hard here with your father?"

"Yes, sir. I am."

"Good. I'm glad to hear that. Tell me, are you going to become a cook, like your father?"

"Oh, no, sir. I'm going to become an engineer and run trains."

"Is that so? Well, we'll have to remember this young man, won't we, Ashenden?"

"We certainly will."

"I'll be right back with your coffee and your desserts, sirs." The empty pitcher in his arms, the boy turned and hurried away.

"If you wish, sir, we can take our coffee inside and look at those blueprints of the bridge at the same time. We won't have much more than forty-five minutes if you want to catch the 3:59 to Sherbrooke."

"Hmm, yes, time waits for no man. I hadn't realized that we had lingered quite so long over lunch."

"If it's fine with you, sir, I won't drive you back to the station but have the older Andosca boy bring you. He has to go to the station to pick up his father's order of foodstuffs at the Express Office."

Chapter 14

In the forty-five minutes before Tyler Andosca arrived to pick him up, Judge Foster and Cyril Ashenden had just enough time to look at the blueprints and also verify their checklist of odds and ends.

While Ashenden was allotted a not insubstantial budget for discretionary spending, for the most part he provided Judge Foster a list of his needs and it was then Foster who placed the orders, and of course, paid the bills. The only exception to this was foodstuffs. Andosca was given almost free rein with respect to daily provisions, and almost all his orders were placed with a wholesaler in Montreal, who in turn billed the OMR Head Office in Eastman.

Food costs were almost regularly over budget, but generally by modest, if not minimal sums. If the judge tolerated the extra expenditure it was because he was fully cognizant of the importance of having a well-nourished work force. The extra money spent on food was saved in other ways, primarily in the rapidity with which the work was being carried out.

It was a great relief to the judge, especially after the fiasco that had occurred two years ago when the project had sputtered and stumbled and eventually stopped altogether.

It had been a mistake to recruit a work crew from the local population, and an even greater mistake to hire workers in proportion to the makeup of the local populace. The linguistic and religious differences—which seemed not to adversely affect the growth and functioning of the towns and villages of the area— somehow made it impossible for the workforce to properly gel into a cohesive unit. The Catholics' insistence on eating fish on Friday—a trivial, inconsequential request from Judge Foster's perspective—became an issue within a matter of weeks. Then, on the feast of the Most Sacred Heart of Jesus, a feast day of which the Judge had previously been blissfully ignorant, half the work force had failed to show up for work. Days later, just as Judge Foster came to the difficult conclusion that his foreman, a jovial but ultimately incompetent Irishman, would have to be let go, the scoundrel ran off with more than a hundred dollars that had been entrusted to him as petty cash for incidentals. These factors, compounded by his wife's failing health (she died in September 1903), prompted the judge to suspend work on the project.

It was a pleasure this year to see how it was progressing, despite the fact that the work had started a little later than had been planned.

"Right now," Ashenden said, "we're three or four days ahead of schedule. The bridge over Salmon Creek shouldn't pose any major problems, as we just saw, and its construction shouldn't take more than five or six weeks. A lot will depend on the weather, on how soon, or how late, snow starts to fall, but if there's no snow before mid-November, which is always possible, we just might start laying rails before winter. If that's the case, the tracks could be fully operational by this time next year, even earlier."

"I don't like to be overly optimistic," the judge replied, "but I must say, I am pleased with what I saw today. It seems we covered as much ground in the last two weeks as we did in the entire month before."

"You're not far off, sir. It's running through bog and wetland that slows us down the most. That, and blasting, of which we've had little to do so far. We will have more coming up, as you saw for yourself. It might be good to order another box or two of dynamite. I have two boxes left but one of those is not full. I think we have enough caps. If I see we don't, I can always send you a telegram, and if we only need a few they are available at the hardware in Windsor. In either case, we haven't reached that outcrop of ledge just yet, and we won't for another four or five days."

"I'll add that to my list, two boxes." In his neat script and using his gold fountain pen, the judge added the item to the dozen or more already on his list: one ton of hay; three hundredweight of oats; two dozen horseshoes and a box of nails; a dozen handles each for picks, shovels, and sledge hammers; a hundredweight of lye soap; four dozen coveralls; one dozen pairs of boots, assorted sizes; one drum of coal oil.

"Last thing, before I forget," said Foster, "what became of the man injured last week?"

"He was sent home, sir. His injuries aren't particularly serious but neither would he be able to work for some time."

"It was logging, as I recall?"

"It was. He was unlucky, too close to a tree that came down. A branch caught him, clipped him and broke his arm, and somehow, the way he fell, he also sprained his knee. We gave him ten dollars compensation, plus all his wages owing, and a ticket back to Albany."

"Lucky, I suppose. All the way around."

"It could have been worse, sir. For him and for us."

"How many men are we down, then?"

"Three in all, since we started."

"You don't want them replaced?"

"I have been considering it, sir, but no. We're making good progress. I haven't really missed the extra hands. As long as we have no other mishaps, we should be in good shape."

"Good, then. I shouldn't tarry too much longer. I don't want to miss my train."

"I'll go call young Andosca."

Judge Foster stood in the shade of Ashenden's tent and reflected on how nicely the last two days had turned out. Gazing south towards Greenlay, he reflected on how astute they had been to proceed with the construction as they had. Originally, the proposal had been to begin by building the bridge over Salmon Creek. By starting in Kingsbury, Orford Mountain Railway trains would be bringing the ties and rails right to the work site. It was on second thought that Ashenden and he—and later the rest of the Board of Governors—opted to do otherwise, to begin clearing the path and building up the subgrade at the opposite end of the spur, at Greenlay.

There were benefits to this second plan. One was that there would be much less initial capital expenditure on materials. The first step, clearing a thirty-foot swath through the forest, would require only manpower (and provided a very small return on labour costs in the form of wood to be sold later). The second step, laying down a four-foot thick bed of rock, gravel and sand, entailed only a minimal cost: that of excavating and hauling from the sand beds and gravel beds that were banked conveniently on the valley floor, where half of the spur would run. The other benefit, more important in the long run, would be that the sub grade would have a winter to shift and settle under the weight of ten feet of snow. If any were to be needed, repairs would be far easier to do before putting the ballast and ties and rails in place.

Judge Foster was brought back from his reverie by the sound of a wagon approaching.

He shook hands goodbye with Ashenden, and, as he climbed up on the wagon, took out his gold watch to check the time.

"Don't worry, sir, we'll be at the train station in plenty of time."

"That's good, young man. Which of the sons are you?"

"Tyler, sir. I'm the second oldest, almost seventeen."

"I believe you work with your father in the kitchen."

"Yes, sir."

"Are you going to be a cook then, like your father?"

"No, sir. I'm going to be a chef."

The judge smiled and reflected on the distinction for a minute before changing the subject. "Tell me, Tyler, what happened to your cheekbone? You seem to have quite a bruise there."

"Oh, that's nothing, sir. It's going to clear up in a couple of days."

"I'm sure it will. But how did you get it? It almost looks as if you've been in a fight."

"Oh, no! No, sir. No, I was in the lean-to stable and the horse shifted over and knocked me off balance and my head got a little banged up when I fell against the wagon that was parked too close."

Chapter 15

Judge Foster made himself as comfortable as he could on the rough boards that served as a seat on the heavy work wagon. Under other circumstances the discomfort of the wooden planks might have been bothersome, but the judge was feeling very serene, very much at peace with the world. The last two days had provided good news on all fronts; even the weather had been perfect: blue sky, pleasantly warm, just enough of a breeze to keep his skin refreshed and insects at bay. In his expansive mood, he was glad to engage Tyler Andosca in conversation, especially since he was such a personable young man.

As the judge had grown older, he'd become more and more interested in family traits. He was conscious that this was an ironic interest on his part, since two of the four children who called him father, were not of his seed. Yet, within his own generation, in addition to his four brothers he had numerous cousins, on both sides of the family, and on both sides of the international border. As well there were their numerous offspring, and increasingly, their offsprings' offspring.

There had been a very large family gathering some five years before and physical traits—a thick mane of hair, a particular set of the jaw—kept turning up, not in every individual certainly, but nevertheless among a considerable number. He'd noticed some rather odd peculiarities. For example, his cousin Minnie from Hartford had always had a slightly grating, high pitched voice and had passed it down two generations to two of her five children and to several grandchildren as well. Within his own family, two of his siblings had followed his father's professional career, and both his brother doctors had at least one son who had similarly become doctors.

Listening to Tyler Andosca, he could hear some of the lilt of the younger brother, Ralph, the young waiter who had charmed him at lunch. He'd noticed on an earlier visit that the four Andoscas who worked in the camp kitchen all bore a striking resemblance to one another. And this son, at least, seemed interested in following in his talented father's culinary footsteps. When he asked if Tyler's paternal grandfather was also a cook, he was not entirely surprised that Tyler had never met the man. After all, Andosca spoke with an immigrant's rather heavy accent, even if his boys did not, but he was surprised by what he did hear, that as a young teenager, Andosca had run away from home and then been shanghaied.

This was not information that Andosca had shared when the judge had interviewed the cook in his cousin's offices in Albany several months before. Andosca had told him only that he had learned to cook on board a ship. "At first, no cook. Wash dishes. Scrub pots. Fetch coal keep stoves hot. But see everything. Learn by look. One day cook assistant have accident, cut hand bad with knife and no work. So I work for two. Easy work: peel potato, cut carrot—not hard. I learn more. Then we in Amsterdam three day, four day. Cook get off boat, go visit, not come back. I there. I start cook. Later, we in America, Boston City. I get off boat. I stay Boston City. Work a little bit here, little bit there. Money good when cook for work men, so I cook. Good life. Winter, three month, depend, spend home with wife. Spring come, somewhere is always someone build railroad. Need cook always. Is no man live no eat. I good cook. Many years experience. Now I do with sons. Ralph twelve year old, I want him come for summer, for two month. Big boy, smart boy. No trouble boy. Work with me. Learn to do. Other boys, older, work like men. Need to pay salary, but Ralph, this year he work for me. No pay salary."

Andosca had good references, among others, that of Judge Foster's cousin. The man was likable, and if he was as good a cook as his cousin claimed, Samuel Foster quite approved of having a young apprentice in the camp kitchen, especially since he came at no cost.

"I didn't know that about your father," Judge Foster said to Tyler Andosca.

"Oh. Maybe I shouldn't have mentioned that. I'd appreciate it if you didn't tell him that I told you, sir."

"I won't say a word. Not that it's anything to be ashamed of. It seems to me that many men who excel do so in the face of adversity. What's that expression? What doesn't kill you makes you stronger."

"Yes, I've heard that before, sir."

"Tell me more about your father."

"Well, he grew up in Italy at a difficult time. This was before Italy was unified. There were a lot of city states and principalities, and there was Garibaldi who wanted to unify the country. Young men were being conscripted to fight for one army or another. Gangs roamed the countryside kidnapping almost anyone who was young and able bodied."

Chapter 16

Francesco fended off branches with one arm and, in the almost total darkness, felt for the trunk with his other outstretched hand. He knew, almost right away by the ridges on the bark that this was probably an olive tree. He turned to let his back fall against its trunk. He would rest for a minute. He had to. His lungs felt as if they were on fire. He gulped in the cool, mountain air to try to douse the heat that seemed to consume him entirely. Breath after breath, his torso heaved with every greedy gulp of cold air. His legs too were aflame, the muscles of his thighs and calves spent almost to exhaustion.

He shifted position and for a minute or two he remained half-bent over, with his hands on his knees, a position of rest, and then he let one knee fall to the ground. He knew he mustn't stop long, even though there was nothing his body would have wanted more than to lay down, even here on rough ground. Rest was the command his lungs and legs were bellowing. But he mustn't, and as if to confirm and to stress the point, he heard a voice. It was distant and seemed to come from far below. The words themselves were unclear and indistinct, but he knew one man was yelling to another to establish his position as they combed their way uphill.

He had to continue. Still, he gave himself time to rub his palms against his thighs and calves, and to take another few deep breaths. He was in an olive grove, and he tried to visualize which one, because there were three of them above the village on the mountain, planted asymmetrically who knew how many centuries ago.

He was certain that this grove could not be the one nearest the village. He had been running far too long for that. He dared hope that this was the one furthest up. But if so, he would now have to traverse to his left. Not far above this grove was an insurmountable barrier, a solid wall of rock that rose vertically. Francesco had once had the impression that if the mountain were an immense prosciutto, the cliff would have been the result of a giant blade slicing off a portion. Further to the left, if he kept climbing, was the narrow pass that would lead him over the mountain and into the next valley, to Ne. If he could get to Ne, to the rail line, he could get to Genoa. But first he had to get to the pass.

He turned uphill, with his arms as much as his eyes guiding him, going to the left any time a tree forced him to make a choice until he got out of the olive grove, climbing what he visualized as a long diagonal line.

Francesco stopped twice more before he reached the pass, and neither time when he listened in perfect stillness and with his full concentration, did he hear human voices carried uphill in the night air. Yet he continued to climb as fast as his legs could push his arms and torso forward. Then, quite suddenly, he was aware that the incline he had been climbing had greatly decreased. A moment later he realized that he was on almost level ground. He stopped then and let himself fall. He lay still with his limbs extended and only his chest moving, heaving with every breath. He lay still for a long time, listening to the pulse of life in the sounds that hummed in the night air. Aside from his own breathing, among all the other sounds that filled the air, he did not hear a single one that he could identify as human. He lay still on the ground until he could no longer feel the blood throbbing in his temples, until his lungs expanded and deflated all but imperceptibly. Eventually, he became aware that the ground under his back was cool, almost cold. Still, he did not move.

He would continue. He would continue downhill towards Ne. But he would wait a little. He was quite sure they'd given up, and so there was no need to keep running. He would wait until first light, and then he would continue. This place was as good as any to rest until then. He knew that going downhill could also be difficult, could present dangers. What if, on this side of the mountain, there was also a cliff, as there was on the side he knew. All his life he had gazed up in wonder at a cliff-face that was called *Il salto dell'angelo*, Angel's Leap. He could imagine, in the darkness, arriving at the top of a precipice even a tenth as high and stepping into fatal emptiness. He would wait until there was enough light to see by. He had not struggled so hard to escape just to die foolishly the moment that he had obtained his freedom.

He was startled awake into a damp, grey mist that seemed to be hiding darker forms, and for a fraction of a second he did not know where he was. Then the darker shapes turned into tree trunks and somewhere overhead the piercing cry that had woken him was repeated. It was the cry of a bird, although he could not identify what species it might be. Francesco sat up and blinked his eyes fully open. The night before came back to him and he understood that he was on top of the mountain, or rather on its shoulder, in the gap that he had raced for and reached. Now it was the break of day. He was surprised that he had fallen asleep. He felt something close to embarrassment. But now that he was awake, he felt refreshed, as if he'd had a good night's sleep in his pallet above the stable.

He stood and looked around. He was in a grove of hardwoods, large trees with leaf-laden branches that let little light down to the forest floor, so there was little in the way of shrubbery and undergrowth. He found that he had spent the night in a small hollow, soft with the humus of decomposed leaves. Above, the full foliage of summer blocked out all but occasional glimpses of the grey sky above, which appeared and disappeared according to the very slight breeze that blew through the high branches. There was still no real light in the sky and all Francesco saw was small, ever-changing patches of grey beyond the blackness of the forest canopy.

In the light mist that shrouded him, he felt quite lost. He knew that he had to travel west, but until the sun started to rise, he'd be unable to tell with certainty where it lay. He had a sense that he was already facing the right way, facing the downhill slope that he wanted to take, but it was better to make sure. There was nothing to do but to wait.

As are all men who work the land—and he had been doing a man's work in fields and barns and ditches and vineyards since he was eight years old—Francesco was accustomed to waiting. The sun would rise soon enough; he was accustomed to rising early, to witnessing the break of dawn. He looked at the faint cloud of vapour he was creating as he exhaled; he hadn't imagined how cool it was this high up the mountain. He was now aware of the early morning cold and an involuntary shiver ran the length of his back. He would be moving soon enough, he told himself, and he would eventually warm up.

He rose and took a few steps in one direction, and then another, making himself familiar with the space around him. There were no clues—none easily visible in the faint, pre-dawn light—to confirm his bearings, his innate sense of the cardinal points. He would soon be moving down hill, but for now he moved to keep warm. He stepped from trunk to trunk in an approximate circle, never more than five or six meters from the spot where he had slept the night. The movement made him think, and he had much to think about.

He had made it up to the pass and he was now safe. He had made it with the clothes on his back—dark canvas trousers that didn't quite reach his ankles, and a cotton shirt that had once been lighter in colour than it was now; he was barefoot, as he had always been. His one possession was a knife that was still safely tucked in the right-hand pocket of his pants, wrapped in a scrap of cloth. It was almost new, with a short blade that folded back into the handle. In the left-hand pocket he had a large blue handkerchief, and deep in the pocket he found a pinch of bread crusts that he popped in his mouth and savoured between his tongue and his pallet until they melted. His last meal had been the previous day at noon, but he was not yet especially hungry. His body was accustomed to labouring for two hours or more before taking any kind of nourishment; nor had last night been the first time that he had gone to bed without supper. Still, he would have been glad for some water.

He was free, but now he was conscious that there would be a cost to his freedom. One part of that cost was that there was no convenient pump where he could get a few cupped handfuls of water. He hoped that he would come across a stream or a rivulet somewhere on his way down the mountain.

When dawn broke and he set off, he was immediately glad that he had not set off in darkness. Within a few dozen strides, Francesco felt the slope start to change, and immediately after, he found himself on a very steep pitch. He descended slowly and carefully, at one point retracing his steps in search of an alternate passage. He traversed, first one way, then the other so that his leg muscles took turns straining against gravity. He moved downhill haltingly, at times using all four limbs to negotiate an unexpectedly steep drop, or a rocky outcrop.

It was on a rock face that Francesco found a thin trickle of water. He stood on a relatively wide ledge, put his mouth against the rock and hungrily pulled at the thin stream, wishing it was the forceful gush of water that came from the mouth of the pump just outside the stable. He stood there for several minutes, seeking to get his fill of water, then leaning his cheeks and forehead against the moist rock face. His feet grew cold on the wet ground and he moved on, only a little refreshed.

Then the vegetation began to change and suddenly he was in a thicket of pines, where the going was difficult in a different way. The slope here was much less steep, but the conifers were growing densely together, their needle-tipped branches forming an intimidating, almost impenetrable, wall. He crouched down, under the prickly limbs. The ground was a soft carpet of needles that had suffocated all vegetation, including the lowest branches of the trees themselves. These thin, dead sticks protruded like spears from every trunk, so that he had to crouch down awkwardly and crawl like a crab to pass as best he could between the evenly spaced trunks. He considered going back up and trying to find a way around the pines. But he had noticed that the trees were growing in perfect symmetry, and that they were all the same size. He was in a plantation and he reasoned that it could not take that much longer to get to the downhill side of it.

Several minutes later, he stepped into a clearing under a sky that had now become an uncertain shade of blue. He couldn't tell, from the light in the overcast sky, how long he'd been making his way down the mountain. He guessed that it was still quite early. The sky seemed to be announcing rain.

He looked around and realized that he was at the edge of a work site. The pines he had been struggling to get through had been harvested here. Dozens and dozens of tree stumps, all cleanly cut some ten centimetres or so above ground level dotted the clearing. There were several large piles of branches, heaped up into pyres to be burned. He noticed there were still a number of limbed trunks waiting to be hauled away, and, twenty meters from where he stood, he saw an opening in the dark pines that must lead, eventually, to the valley floor and the village of Ne, where railway tracks ran west to Genoa.

The opening led to a rough trail that traversed the slope at a relatively shallow pitch, going across the mountain as much as down it, leading south as much as west. It was a narrow trail and the long ruts that scarred the ground showed that it had served to haul logs out of the clearing. It was easy going compared to his descent so far, and for a moment he felt as if he were almost floating on air.

But Francesco had not gone more than a few dozen meters when he was startled by a sound. He immediately left the trail and took several steps into the woods before he stopped, turned, squatted low, and waited to see what it was that had startled him. A moment later he heard voices and then saw two men. They trudged in single file with their heads and torsos bent forward, intent on their upward march, engrossed in their desultory conversation. Only for a moment could Francesco make out actual words, although not enough to form an idea of what they might have been discussing. The second man was leading a mule lightly packed with tools: axes, saws, shovels, ropes. Then the woodcutters' voices faded as quickly as they had come, and after a minute, Francesco stepped back onto their logging trail.

He came into another clearing where the first thing he noticed was the sky. He was struck by its strange hue, neither grey nor blue, but a nameless, lifeless colour. He hoped it would not rain.

Then he noticed the goats. They had perceived him first, so that when he saw them, he found himself looking into half a dozen pairs of large, inquisitive eyes. The animals were tethered, and by the absence of vegetation in clearly defined circles, it was easy to see the spots where they had been previously tied to a peg driven into the ground. After a moment, the goats went back to their grazing.

He scanned the clearing and saw two openings on its down-hill side. He could sense the valley below by the emptiness above the tree line, but even though he found himself at the highest point in the clearing, he could see that he would have to climb several meters to be able to look into the valley below. He considered climbing a tree, but although there were countless trees, none in his immediate vicinity lent itself to an easy climb.

Where the trail forked in the clearing, he looked back the way he had come. There was a wall of woods, behind which treetops climbed steeply to a trough between two peaks. He knew what he was looking at even if it was totally foreign. As he looked uphill, the forest seemed dark, and hostile. He turned downhill and chose the fork that veered towards the north rather than the south. He had once seen a map and its image had remained very clear in his mind. He knew he was going west, more precisely slightly northwest towards Genoa.

This path through this woodland was a little wider than the logging trail. He had only gone a few meters along it when he was conscious of a sound. He stepped off the path, followed his ears, and a moment later fell to his knees by a small brook and drank again. This was not food, which his stomach was now starting to crave, but it was water, cold, life-giving water. He drank his fill of this water that gushed so much more force-fully—and without any effort on his part—than the water from the pump by the stable. He splashed the cold water on his face and neck, and when he stood up again, he felt he was a new man.

When he stopped again, not fifty meters further down the trail, it was because of voices. He quickly stepped into the woods but this time, although he waited several minutes, no one came up the path. He continued to hear voices, faintly and intermit-tently, but he couldn't judge how far off they might be, or picture what they might represent. He made his way forward through the woods parallel to the path, moving slowly and quietly. He was curious to see, but reluctant to be seen. He didn't go very far before he found himself at the edge of another clearing, on a small plateau. He realized that he was at the edge of a small field of wheat. In the middle of the field, working their way up towards him, were four labourers harvesting the grain, and one of them was singing as he swung his scythe. He ducked several meters back into the woods, then turned and began traversing his way through the trees, to circumvent the field.

Half an hour later, he found himself on a small bluff, and he was able to see out over the valley into which he was descending. Below him, on a slope that grew more and more gradual, was a chessboard of forests and fields. There were olive groves, recognizable by the dull grey-green of their foliage, and orchards; some he knew would now be laden with fruit. There were vineyards. There were fields of grain, and pastureland. Scattered on this landscape were houses, stables, granaries, sheds. These all grew more concentrated on the valley floor where only a few stands of trees still stood. He knew that a river flowed through the valley, although from where he stood, it was all but hidden, and only at one spot could he see a glimpse of it. He was expecting to see the town of Ne, but there was no sign of it, neither upstream nor down. This puzzled him but didn't worry him. It was not difficult to imagine that a town stood not far away.

As if to confirm his suspicion, he heard what he thought must be the tolling of church bells, though he could see no steeple. The sound was very faint, but unmistakable, and he now knew the direction to Ne. He couldn't tell from the sky what time it might be, and he wondered for a minute if it was noon and the bells were sounding the Angelus. He listened and concluded that the bells were ringing for a special mass, or a funeral.

The second thing that puzzled him, and this was more worrisome, was the railway that was supposed to be there. He could see no sign of one; however, he could see small parts of one or two roads. He told himself that, from this distance, if he could hardly see a river, he should not be surprised that he could not see train tracks. He wondered if they were on this side of the river, or on the other. He studied the panorama that lay before him for another few minutes, looking for the easiest path to the valley floor.

When the Angelus rang very faintly some time later, Francesco found himself at the edge of another clearing, an orchard of neatly aligned plum trees that were being harvested by at least three people, as best he could judge by the voices. As the church bells began tolling, the one woman he could see stopped, and bowed her head in prayer. Francesco realized that he should too and he fell to one knee, as if in atonement, and bowed his head as well, but he immediately raised his eyes when the bells stopped to see if the woman would leave the orchard, and by what way.

She had disappeared. She had gone, he assumed, to join the others, but if they were near or far, he had to wait to tell. He could see no one, but he was aware of their faint voices, and he imagined that the fruit pickers were seated somewhere, eating whatever food they might have brought with them for their mid-day meal.

He could hear his stomach rumbling faintly. Francesco was understandably hungry. He had eaten nothing for almost twenty-four hours. If he could see no one, it seemed reasonable that no one could see him. He stepped out of the woods and into the orchard, looking around, to be sure that he really was alone, at least in this part of the orchard. He took a plum from a tree. The fruit was ripe, and with no effort he split the plum open to remove the pit and he put both halves into his mouth at once.

The plum was sweet, and juicy, and he savoured it fully. The next several plums went into his pockets. Who knew when he would next find food? Good as the plums were, he ate no more than a dozen. He knew it would not do to gorge too much on fruit. He had eaten enough to appease his stomach for a while. He stepped back into the woods where, unseen, he circumvented the orchard and continued his downhill trek until he had left the faint voices behind.

But he didn't go far. He had been walking, if not scrambling or crawling, since dawn. He had no idea how far he might have come, nor any idea how much further it was to Ne, the first destination he had set for himself. He had eaten, and even though it was only plums, they constituted a strangely satisfying meal. He found what looked like a comfortable spot under an oak and looked around even though he knew that he was quite alone. He lay down carefully so as not to damage his small hoard of plums, curled up as best he could, and within minutes fell asleep.

He was startled awake by a grunt. He sat up, confused, unaware for an instant where he was. A second grunt made him turn his head, and he found himself looking at a wild boar no more than two meters away. Francesco kept still for a moment, and then thrust his head forward the little he could and hissed loudly at the animal.

It jumped back several meters, and Francesco was on his feet. He cursed the plums in his pocket because they prevented him from reaching his knife. But he saw that he was lucky. It wasn't a fully-grown animal, rather a half-grown adolescent. He kept his eyes on the wild boar that was staring back at him, albeit now from a safer distance. He slowly reached his right hand into his pocket and took out a plum. Still moving slowly, he crouched just a little, and drew his arm back to be able to throw with force. At the same instant he leapt up, yelled loudly and threw the plum at the animal.

It turned and ran, and even as he felt relief, he wondered if the boar might still be with its mother, if there might be several other animals nearby. He stood in place for a few minutes, to get his bearings before continuing on. He couldn't tell how long he might have been sleeping. It felt quite late, but he wondered if that was because it was such an overcast day, and the forest canopy all but blocked out the light. Perhaps, he told himself, it wasn't as late as it felt.

He reached into his pocket and pulled out two plums that he ate slowly and deliberately, savouring the meaty green flesh that tasted sweet and felt cool on his tongue. He continued eating plums as he made his way downhill through the stand of mixed hardwoods. He took the plums, one by one, from the pocket in which he kept his knife, until there was only one left. He kept that one for later, even though his other pocket was still half-full. The plums were good, but whatever satisfaction his body had taken from them had given way to a desire for other food, a variety of food as opposed to a greater quantity of plums.

He resolutely set his mind to not think about food; instead, he pictured the valley as he had seen it from the bluff. Certain that he had followed the course he had set for himself, he anticipated coming out of these woods, and crossing pastures and fields on his way towards the river and—he hoped—the railway track. Unavoidably, he would see people and be seen by them. If he was lucky, he would come across a footpath, or a road, so that he could continue on quickly and without attracting any attention. A stranger passing by on a public road is of little interest and little consequence; a stranger trespassing on a man's plot of land is a source of suspicion, and unlikely to receive a warm welcome.

He jumped, his heart pounding with adrenaline, shocked out of his thoughts by a sound he had never before heard but that he recognized half a moment later. Somewhere below, a train was blowing its whistle. He could see no sign of the train—his view blocked by trunks and branches—but he was immensely encouraged by the sound. He moved a little faster.

He cautiously stepped out of the woods and into a small pasture where a donkey and two dozen sheep were grazing. To one side, beyond a row of Lombardy poplars that defined the neighbour's demarcation, there were stone buildings that were likely sheds or stables. Turning the other way where the vegetation was largely low, and rather scraggly, he found that the greenery was hiding a ditch, and on the other side, beyond what grew wild, was a field that had recently been harvested, and was now covered in golden stubble. Beyond the field, a few hundred meters away, were buildings: a farmhouse, a stable, and sheds. There was an orchard, and gardens. He counted three people, and then a fourth.

A woman came out of the house, walked a few dozen meters and then disappeared into a small mound. A few minutes later, she reappeared, this time carrying something that she brought into the house. Again, Francesco's hunger returned. He could picture the root cellar that the woman had entered. No doubt it was half-full of food: cured hams, salamis, sausages, cheeses, olives, dried fruit, what might remain of last year's root vegetables. It would be foolish, with so many people around, to attempt to get into that root cellar. For a moment, he considered approaching the house to beg.

Before he could make a decision, for the second time in what couldn't have been more than an hour, he heard the train whistle. It was considerably louder than the first time, and even though he could not see the train, he was able to follow its progress by a plume of grey smoke that appeared above the tree line. The sound was enough to make Francesco start moving again. He stayed at the edge of fields and pastures where there were windbreaks, or stone walls, or ditches harbouring vegetation.

He moved steadily, his eyes constantly scanning, doing as much work as his feet and legs. He occasionally looked back over his shoulder, just in case, but also to gage how far he had distanced himself from the mountain. Then, quite suddenly, he was on a road, on a public road where he felt no longer the hunted animal. He straightened his back and shoulders, raised his head. He was alone on the road, at least for now, but here he felt that he was again among people, a new people where no one knew him, making of him a new man. Here he felt freer than he had up on the mountain the night before.

For the third time that day, he heard a bell tolling, and he knew it was now six o'clock. That surprised him because the dull sky made it seem much later. He didn't stop to bow his head in prayer, though he did make the sign of the cross. He continued on, not knowing exactly where he might be going, but knowing that he had to hurry before he was caught by the promised downpour. The sky to the west was now an ominous grey, streaked with angry slabs of slate-black clouds that promised a hard, pummelling rain. Still, as he hurried on, he told himself he had been lucky, for the sky had been promising rain all day, and he had made it to the valley floor without getting soaked.

He came to a road that seemed to run roughly north to south, and he turned north, towards where he imagined Ne to be. Now and again, he saw smaller lanes that led to small farms, sometimes near enough that the houses and farm buildings were visible, sometimes not. He crossed an old man in a cart being drawn by a mule. Francesco continued walking briskly, and as he passed the man, he nodded his head, as if greeting an acquaintance. The old man stared at Francesco suspiciously but returned a barely perceptible nod. He passed a dozen others as well, men and women whom he took to be farm hands, people who seemed to be much like him, and none seemed any more friendly than the old man. All seemed to be returning from fields or orchards, some carrying scythes, or rakes, or shovels.

Then he was alone again on the road. For a moment, on a rise in the road, he caught a glimpse of a church steeple and wondered how far ahead it might be. The church, Francesco knew, was a sanctuary. There he would find at least shelter from the rain. But he went no more than a few hundred meters when he felt the first drop.

There were trees along the road that might have provided an imperfect shelter, but Francesco wanted something better, and despite the potential danger, he turned into the nearest lane and, half crouched to make himself as small as possible, ran towards the nearest farm building. He reached it just as the intermittent drops turned into a steady and heavy downpour. By keeping his back flat against the building's stone wall, he could stay under the overhanging eaves and so remain at least partially dry. He was hidden from the farmhouse and so he remained there, leaning against the wall to rest as much as he could even though he was still on his feet, which were growing cold as the rain turned dust and dirt to cold mud. He looked up and saw a sky that hung low and dark over his head. With the rain, came cold, but Francesco stayed put despite his shivering. Only when night had completely fallen did he edge his way to the corner of the building.

Tentatively, he poked his head around the corner. From where he stood, he could see the farmhouse some thirty meters away, as well as two other sheds. A faint, flickering light shone from two of the ground-floor windows of the house. Unsurprisingly, there was no one in sight, and if there was a dog, it too was hiding in some sheltered spot. He stepped around the corner and immediately felt the rain beat down on him. It took him no more than a few seconds to reach a door but that was long enough for the rain to soak him to the skin.

He was lucky. The door was held closed by no more than a simple latch, and he quickly stepped inside out of the rain and immediately pushed the door closed behind him. The darkness was almost absolute, but he could tell immediately by the smells that he was in a stable. He could hear that his arrival had provoked a slight stirring; animals that had been asleep, or at rest, rose, or turned or shuffled in their pens or stalls. And then he heard something else, a low growl emanated from somewhere deep in the darkness.

He could see nothing. He listened, his every fibre taut with concentration. He heard a pig's sleepy, half-hearted grunt, a cow's or perhaps a mule's inquisitive snuffle, a chicken's confused cackle, and again the unmistakable growl of a large dog. Francesco had always been told that dogs can smell fear, and he knew that now he must not be fearful. Yet he was.

He reached into his pocket, pulled out his knife, and opened it. He crouched, to make himself as small as possible, and put one knee to the ground to make himself as solid and stable as possible. Clutching his knife with his right hand, and with his right arm half-extended, he waved his small weapon in front of him.

And then, softly, he began to sing.

Nina nana bel bambin
Notte scada stami vicin
Sta vicin bimbo mio
Sta vicin e pregha Dio

It was an old and comforting lullaby and he repeated it over and over, like a mantra. He continued long after there were no sounds at all, other than that of his own soft voice. He rose slowly and switched his knife from his right hand to his left. He retreated half a step so that his back was against the stable door. With his right arm extended, he explored the wall with his hand. Slowly, he stepped towards the right. That was where he thought he had heard the hens protesting.

It took him several minutes but eventually his outstretched hand touched feathers, and he immediately received a nasty peck for his trouble. The bird emitted a squawk, which elicited a brief chorus from several other birds. Francesco put his knife away. Using both hands—one to push the hen slightly off her nest and the other to search the straw. Ignoring the occasional pain inflicted by an angry beak, he searched one nest after the other. In all, he collected three eggs from seven chickens. These he ate, first cracking the shell and then pulling it open above his raised head so the contents would fall directly into his open mouth.

As he was swallowing the last of the eggs, he became aware again of the dog as a presence at his hip. The animal had not growled but had come silently to investigate. He was conscious of the dog's cold nose inspecting him. Francesco remained calm, and again began softly singing the lullaby. The dog didn't growl, and after a minute, satisfied by its olfactory examination, it retreated into the darkness.

While the three eggs were neither filling nor tasty, Francesco knew that they were providing at least a little nutrition. Had there been more, he would have gladly eaten those as well. He finished his meal with the last of his fruit.

Again, feeling his way in the dark, he worked his way back to the door and let himself slip to the dirt floor right next to it. He would rest here. Should the barn's owner arrive unexpectedly, he might be able to quickly scoot out the door and, with his young legs, outrun a farmer, especially if the man were old.

He awoke aware that something was different. It was still dark. He was conscious of something warm up against his body and realized that it was the dog. Something else had awoken him. He remained perfectly still and listened until it came to him: the absence of the sound of rain. He had no way of knowing what time it might be. Once his eyes had accustomed themselves to the darkness, he noticed a small rectangle on the opposite wall that was somehow a different shade of black. He looked at it now, aware that it was a window, curious to see if it betrayed any sign of light. It did, but it was the very faint glow of a clear night sky. He lay still for a few minutes, absorbing the dog's warmth, knowing that the rain would have left behind cold air, and a wet, muddy road. But he also knew it was best to leave now, even if daybreak was an hour or two away, though he wondered if the sun might not rise even sooner.

He softly hummed the lullaby and sang it quietly one more time for his bed mate before getting up. He rose with slow, unhurried calm, and spoke to the dog that he couldn't see but that he knew was somewhere next to him, "Thanks for sharing your room. I wish I could offer you something by way of payment." He found the door latch with his hand. "You stay here," he told the dog, suspecting that the dog too might want its liberty. He slipped out into the cold night air, being careful that the door was securely latched behind him.

The sky was clear and sparkling with stars. The moon was still up, half-full, providing almost enough light to see by. He stood still for a minute, with his back against the stable door, and surveyed the farmhouse and the farmyard by the faint moonlight. There was no sign of life anywhere, no lights, no movement. Sometimes farmers kept a second dog that roamed loose at night. Francesco hoped that this farmer didn't, but he took out his knife and opened it, just in case. He stood by the stable door for a few more minutes until he was able to make out, in the half-light of the night sky, what he hoped he would find: a small tell-tale mound indicating the presence of a root cellar.

The light that came in through the open door was so faint that Francesco explored the root cellar by touch and by smell more than by sight. He found garlic sausages. He took his knife and cut one from the cord by which it hung suspended from a rafter and slid it into his pocket. He cut a second and then third sausage to fill one pocket. He found hams, cheeses, salamis. He decided quickly and he took a salami, one small enough to fit in his other pocket. With these provisions, as much as he could carry in his pockets, he turned and left. He was careful to close the door. He glanced once at the shrouded, sleeping farmhouse, and silently made his way to the barn, to the laneway, and back to the road. Not until then did he pull a sausage out of his pocket and begin to eat.

He walked as he ate, although after the first two bites, he made a point of eating slowly. Now that he had food, more food than he could possibly eat in one sitting, he wanted to savour it. This was sustenance, but it brought enjoyment and he wanted to stretch the enjoyment out. He was taking the last few bites of the sausage when dawn broke.

When the Angelus rang, Francesco was taking his first steps on the creosote railway ties that led westward. He had been lucky, he realized, for the tracks ran on his side of the river.

It was difficult walking. He was barefoot and he wanted to avoid the crushed stones with their sharp points and razor edges that separated the ties. But the ties were set closer together than was comfortable for his natural stride. He found it clumsy taking short steps from one tie to the next, but almost as awkward trying to step on every second tie. In either case, walking took concentration. Slow but sure, he told himself, slow but sure. He was grateful for the weather: the sky had broken a clear blue, the air fresh and cool. The railway tracks ran very straight and very level. Step by step he stuttered through a patchwork of fields and forests; occasionally the track ran quite close to a farmyard sheltered behind a row of poplars. Eventually he began to see people working in fields and knew that he too might well be seen. He kept his steady, silent pace; he posed no harm to those he saw; he was of no more than passing interest to them, and he soon slipped out of their sight. Now and again he had a view of the river to his right.

He had continued with small, stumbling steps for some time before he finally had a chance to drink. His thirst had begun a moment after he took his last bite of sausage and had been growing ever since. He had seen one or two small streams running through culverts under the tracks, but they'd been too close to farmyards. Here, the rill ran through woodland. He braved the crushed stones to make his way down to a swollen brook. He drank, and then drank some more, and then washed his face and neck. He found a place to sit, ten meters from the tracks, where he leaned as comfortably as he could against a tree trunk, opened his knife and cut a generous slice of salami for himself. He thought it must be close to mid-morning. He tried to estimate how far he might have travelled and tried to picture how far he might still have to go. For the moment, he was sated, and out of the sun, under the quiet of softly rustling branches, near a murmuring stream.

He was startled to his feet by a fearsome noise that he could not immediately identify but that was amplified with every heartbeat, coming closer and closer, and only when it thundered over the culvert, ten meters away did Francesco see a train for the first time in his life. He was in awe. It was a monstrous beast that chugged clouds of steam and smoke. It ran on great metal wheels that rolled by faster than any horse could possibly gallop, and pulled oversized wagons and carriages, four times the size of any wagon or carriage he had ever seen, and these were almost too many to count as they too rumbled quickly by on metal wheels that were small only by comparison to the giant wheels of the engine.

Francesco took stock of his situation. It was now noon, or very close to it, with the sun strong and high overhead; it was not the best time of day to be out walking. Still, Francesco felt rested, and there was little reason to stay where he was. He cut two more slices of salami and ate them slowly, then went back to the stream and drank his fill. Who could say when he might find water again? Rather than climb back to the tracks where he would be exposed to the full heat of the sun, he set off walking along the edge of the clearing that marked the rail line's right of way. If it wasn't easier walking, at least it was no harder, and he was in partial shade at least some of the time.

An hour or so later, Francesco found the track veering in a long, slow curve towards the right. Then the land started to fall away while the tracks continued straight and level, above him. He braved the painful points and edges of the ballast to climb up to the tracks. Here he could see that they continued as if through mid air over a trestle bridge spanning a river. He could not yet see the river from where he was, but sensed that he would not have too far to go to reach it. And when he got there, how could he cross it? He, who did not swim. Yet the danger on the tracks was all too evident: the bridge spanned the river and part of the river valley. Once he was on the bridge, he would have to cover a quarter of a kilometre or more to reach the other side, and over that long stretch, there would be no getting off the tracks. If a train suddenly came, there would be no place to take refuge until it passed by. He would be in its path and it would crush him more easily than he could crush an ant with his foot. How long would it take him to cover that distance? When would a train come by? He hesitated.

There was no immediate reason for Francesco to hesitate, just as there was no reason to start crossing right away. As if to emphasise the point, he paused where he was and cut first one, and then a second slice of salami, and studied the bridge in front of him. It was a sight beyond anything he had ever imagined. He stared down the tracks and saw that after they crossed the bridge, they curved westward again to run along the opposite bank.

Eventually, he ventured a few dozen meters towards the bridge but then stopped. Some sixth sense was holding him back.

A few minutes later he heard it, and then saw it. He quickly scrambled down the rock-strewn embankment. A train, this time Westbound, roared by as Francesco stood twenty meters away, his mouth half open in wonder. He watched it pass and stared as it shrank in size and eventually disappeared. He made the sign of the cross, touching his right hand to his forehead, his chest, his left and then right shoulders. He climbed back up to the tracks, the soles of his feet enduring as best they could the crushed rock that served as ballast for the rail bed, and started to follow the departed train across the trestle bridge.

A moment later the crushed stone between the railway ties disappeared and Francesco found himself looking at vegetation that was sloping downhill so that with every step he was higher and higher above the ground. He forced himself to go on, slowly and methodically. He realized that he must not look down, that he must put his entire focus on the next railway tie and will himself not to see the ever-growing drop through empty space. He was aware of the river when he reached it and felt a tremendous relief a few hundred steps later when he became aware that he was again over vegetation. When he was almost to the other side, he stopped, lifted his eyes and looked first upstream at the valley he had so far travelled, and then toward the valley downstream where he was going. Francesco was not insensitive to the natural beauty of the forests that rose from the river valley and up the foothills towards the mountains that defined the skyline. For a moment, he felt as if the entire world was his.

He saw one spire, and a few minutes later, a second spire, and knew before he got there that this was a much larger place than the only village he had ever known in his short life. It was settled into a much broader valley nestled between lower, rounder mountains than those he had left. He knew intuitively to abandon the tracks that had brought him this far, crossed an empty pasture, and stepped onto a well-worn road.

There were more houses than he had ever before seen. Some of them were behind wrought iron fences and others behind stone walls interrupted by large coach doors. Then the houses rose from the edge of the street, two and three storeys high, with steps leading up to their solid doors that were flanked by large, half-shuttered windows. The street opened onto a square lined by shops and stores, and dominated by a large church. In the middle of the square was a small oasis of greenery where half a dozen trees provided some shade. In the shade were a number of people milling about and Francesco realized that they were gathered around a water pump at the edge of the oasis. Some seemed to be idly gossiping, but others were filling their pails and pitchers with water.

Francesco watched and waited for several minutes, and when the crowd at the pump had largely dispersed, the several women going off in their different directions leaving two old men on a nearby bench, he crossed the square and made his way to the water pump. Francesco was aware that the two men were watching him approach, even though he made a point of not looking in their direction, not till he was half a dozen steps from the pump. He nodded his head towards them in greeting.

"*Buon pomeriggio*," he addressed them. "May I help myself to some water?"

"Of course," said the stouter of the two, "as much as you want."

He worked the pump handle with his right hand, and as the water gushed from the spout, he caught what he could with his cupped left hand and brought the cool liquid to his lips. He drank a dozen handfuls, and then splashed some water over his face and neck.

He was aware that the two men had kept their eyes on him. When he finished, he turned to them and said, "*Grazie*."

"You're welcome," said the stouter of the two.

"Tell us," said the other, "were you just now bringing lambs to Marcello?"

"No," replied Francesco.

"You did not bring a few lambs just around the corner, to Marcello's butcher shop, to be slaughtered?" insisted the old man.

"No," answered Francesco, straightening himself. "I do not know a Marcello."

"Bartolomeo, let the young man be," said the stouter of the two.

"I just asked a question of the young man."

"Excuse my friend, young man. He is an old fogey who reads too many books."

"I beg your pardon if my question offended you," Bartolomeo said to Francesco, and then turned to his companion. "I saw a young man I have not seen before. He is sufficiently out of the ordinary that I am curious about him. The young man is barefoot and is dressed as a shepherd might dress. Further, as he bends over to drink, I see a sausage protruding from his trouser pocket. I ask myself, what would explain this young man being here, in this square, a hundred meters from Marcello's butcher shop if not that he is a shepherd who drove a flock of lambs to be slaughtered, was compensated for his trouble with one of

Marcello's sausages, and stopped for a drink before returning to his home in the hills. That is all. If the young man tells me that no, he has not been to Marcello's, I accept that my deduction was incorrect. And I hope I have not offended the young man."

"You see?" the stouter man addressed Francesco. "This is not my friend Bartolomeo talking. It is the foolish books he reads that come from London."

"Young man," said the other reaching into one of his pockets, "let me apologize to you again. Here take this for the inconvenience I might have caused you. No, no, take it and buy yourself some wine to drink with your sausage. It is a gift to you from a gentleman."

Francesco did not understand everything because the word 'gentleman' had been spoken in English, but the stouter man laughed as if he had heard a joke. Francesco smiled, accepted the coin that had been proffered to him, slightly bowed his head towards the two men, and stepped away, ready to orient himself in a westerly direction.

Then, quite suddenly, Francesco was aware of a group of boys, five of them, hovering nearby. They might have been his age, or close to it, but they were town boys, schoolboys with crisp shirts and knotted ties and satchels or books strapped together with a leather belt. They were staring at him, pointing at him, making comments and then laughing uproariously.

"*Scalzo!*" they yelled at him. "Barefoot peasant!"

They were as well shod as they were well dressed. For the first time Francesco was self-conscious about his shoeless state.

He backed away, looking quickly one way and then the other for an escape route. Their jeering insults hurt him but little, although if one of them alone had confronted him, he might well have taken exception and replied in kind. He was afraid of something else, of an undercurrent of implied violence that he sensed in their posture and voices. He was badly outnumbered, and more than that, he wanted no part of any conflict, only to be on his way.

He backed up a little more, then spun on his heels and walked briskly towards one of the streets that led away from the square. He was not going in the direction that he wanted, but he had little choice at this point. Once he lost this pack of boys, he would re-orient himself and continue westward.

He walked quickly, little aware of his surroundings, focused on getting as far down the street as possible, as far away as possible from the boys behind him. But, by their continued laughter and cries of '*scalzo*,' he knew he was being followed. He turned a corner onto another street, where they followed him, and he turned again at another corner.

Abruptly, he broke into a run. He ran down one street, turned a corner, and ran down another. He was faster than his pursuers who were burdened by books and satchels, and had he known where he was going, he'd have made good his escape, but suddenly, upon turning a corner, he found himself twenty meters down a dead-end street. He had to turn to face his adversaries.

For the five boys, this was a lark, an unexpected game they'd come upon as they made their way home from school. For Francesco, it was a flight for survival. The running had winded the boys more than it had winded Francesco. As well, it had spaced the boys out, the slower ones were now several dozen metres behind their speedier classmates.

When Francesco turned around, he saw the first of his pursuers come around the corner. It was the biggest of the five, the one Francesco had guessed might be the ringleader. Francesco saw that the boy was a little taller than he was, but he also saw that the boy was momentarily surprised. His prey was not twenty meters ahead of him as before, but suddenly only a few meters away. He was surprised as well because, if only for a second, he was alone, having outdistanced his classmates by several metres.

Francesco lowered his head and rammed it with all his force into the boy's chest. Both went down, but it was Francesco who was on his feet a second later when the second boy, and then the third came around the corner. They saw Francesco standing over their fallen classmate. Francesco, making himself as threatening as possible, moved towards the boys, and towards the dead-end street's only way out.

Heedless of their fallen classmate, the two boys turned in time to push the final two laggards back the way they had come. Francesco followed them only as far as the corner, just to be sure that they were still running in the opposite direction.

He turned back to the fallen boy who was still on the ground, gasping for the breath that had so suddenly been knocked out of him. Acting on an impulse that he would not have been able to explain, Francesco dropped knees-first onto the boy's midriff, again knocking the wind out of him. His former tormentor was now all but totally incapacitated. Francesco turned his attention to the boy's shoes. While he had never owned shoes himself, he was not unfamiliar with them, had seen pairs before, seen how their laces could be neatly tied into bows. He quickly untied the laces and just as quickly slipped the boy's shoes off his feet.

Holding his prize, he turned his back on the field of battle where the boy was gasping for breath between sobs.

Carrying a shoe in each hand, Francesco quickly quit the dead-end street, turned in the direction opposite the one the boys had taken, and walked briskly away. Several minutes later he found a street running approximately east west, turned west, and eventually found himself out of the town and back in the countryside where he felt far more comfortable.

At a point where he was quite alone, he sat down and tried to put the shoes on his feet. They did, in fact, fit Francesco, but they felt un-natural and after only a few hundred metres one of the shoes began to chaff his Achilles tendon. Following a Sunday morning custom he'd seen all his life, Francesco tied the laces together and slung the shoes around his neck. He strutted on like an athlete sporting hard won laurels.

Two days later, he was on the docks in Genoa.

Chapter 17

Wasn't it surprising, thought the judge as he pulled his gold watch from his vest and flipped it open, how short a trip can seem with good conversation—or an unexpected story, because Tyler had told his father's story with only occasional comments, queries or exclamations from the judge.

"Don't worry, sir, we've plenty of time. I'm just going to give the horses a little water."

Swinging the bucket he'd lifted from its hook on the side of the wagon, Tyler Andosca stepped briskly around two waiting teams and walked quickly to the spring just up ahead on the side of the road. It was a warm day, and there were three or four people gathered around it, each with a pail, or a bucket, or an ewer come to fetch water.

The judge noted that the southbound train he had to catch was scheduled to arrive in Windsor at 3:47 and pull out—with him aboard—at 3:59. They had a full nineteen minutes before it was due. Even if he had to walk the remaining distance, the judge calculated, he could be on the train before it left the station. Not that he would want to walk. The judge was no longer a young man, and if he had been home, he would almost certainly have stretched out on the sofa and taken a short rest, if not a nap. But he had been outside for a good part of the day and the fresh air was revitalizing and stimulating.

The judge sat back, closed his eyes, and lifted his head skyward to let the sun's heat beat down directly on his face for a minute or two. It was the middle of August, he reminded himself, and the sun-starved month of November would arrive soon enough.

In his mind's eye, he traced the route to his destination in Windsor. They would continue up the River Road for another quarter mile or so, past more than half a dozen properties—one of them, in the Victorian style, was noticeable for being almost new and more substantial than its neighbours. At the Brompton Road they would turn east, cross the bridge, and then go down Main Street less than a quarter mile to the train station.

He'd have a light meal this evening—he had eaten very well outside Ashenden's tent—and then get a good night's sleep. The Three Forks Hotel had always provided him with very restful nights, despite its proximity to the Sherbrooke train station.

He hoped that the last two days were a good augury for tomorrow.

He would be meeting tomorrow morning at ten with Dittson in the rather opulent office of the president of the Eastern Townships Bank on Wellington Street. No doubt Donaldson, the bank's senior vice-president would be there as well, quite possibly along with one or two others. Dittson always liked to have a few of his underlings with him so as to outnumber his client.

Samuel Foster had been dealing with banks for his entire adult life. He had come to several conclusions about banks. One was that they were difficult institutions to live with, but they were equally difficult to live without, unless one lived a hermit's existence and kept one's stash of coppers and dimes hidden in the toe of a sock. Another was that banks were all too eager and anxious to lend one sums of money when one didn't really need a loan but were parsimonious to the extreme those times that one actually was in need of financial assistance.

Judge Foster's present financial state, with respect to the Orford Mountain Railway, was closer to the latter than the former. The judge was far from destitute; in fact, he was one of the richest men in the Eastern Townships, and if the country had had its own aristocracy based on wealth and pedigree, the judge would have been one of its minor members. But even rich men can occasionally find themselves in need of a little more money.

He knew that Dittson would provide the funds the OMR needed, but at what cost? That was the question. The judge had already mortgaged several of his properties. The question was, how many more would the bank demand, and at what rates? The sale of the plot of land in Upper Melbourne—not yet a done deal but the Marcotte brothers seemed almost certain to buy—would also provide a bit of cash.

He was broken out of his reverie by a sharp metallic knock somewhere close to him. It was Tyler Andosca, hooking a now empty pail up to the wagon.

It was a reflex action more than any real curiosity that made the judge again pull his gold watch from his vest pocket and snap it open.

The boy had taken a long time to fetch water for the horses. They'd be at the station well before the final, "On board!" but not with the margin he had expected. As he looked at the boy to ask what had taken so long, he noticed some subtle difference in him, almost as if a glow were emanating from his countenance, certainly from his smile. It was impossible on the wagon seat for the judge to see into young Tyler Andosca's eyes, and he wasn't entirely convinced that they were truly the mirror of the soul, but he was unequivocally certain that the human face reflects inner emotions; even with only a profile view of Tyler Andosca's face there was no doubt in the judge's mind that his young kitchen employee was brimming with joy. The judge was not without innate curiosity, but he held his peace.

Although Foster said nothing, the boy was immediately reassuring, "Don't worry, sir! Don't worry at all. I was a bit longer at the spring, but we'll be at the station in plenty of time."

To make his point, he startled the team to a quick trot for just a moment before slowing down so that the horses were walking at their normal pace when they passed a young woman who was walking with a quick step up the road from the spring, despite the large ewer she carried cradled in her arms. As he drove the wagon past her, Tyler leaned briefly backwards for a moment to make sure the water bucket was well secured on its hook on the wagon's sideboard. The judge couldn't be sure, but he wondered if Tyler had not done so just to catch a better glimpse of the girl.

A moment later, after they went by the red-bricked, Victorian-style house that the judge always noticed on this short stretch of the River Road, he prompted Tyler, "You were telling me how your father took two days to walk to the port of Genoa. I imagine that's where he found work?"

"No, he didn't get the chance to find work. He got to Genoa and he was shanghaied. His last memory was of being near the docks, asking someone for directions. Then, when he woke up, he was in the middle of the Ligurian Sea."

Part 2

Chapter 18

Oh! Shawn! Well done! Everything is working again! We have our screen back! Isn't that good news?

I can stop talking now and get back to the original program which was to present you with all the pieces of the puzzle so you can see for yourselves the solution to the mystery of the Melbourne Murder.

Now, as I look at the time, I think I'll jump directly to the diary.

Although, I did have a few more documents that I had intended to show you. Perhaps it will be quicker if I just summarize them for you briefly.

On the 18th of August, the day after the *Sherbrooke Daily Record* broke the story of the murder, there was a follow-up piece, much shorter of course, but still on the front page.

This second article corrected the name of the boy who had been slain. (You're all familiar with the *Sherbrooke Record* and its reputation for not always getting everything exactly right; as you can see this reputation goes back some ways.) The twelve-year-old's name, the paper stated, was Ralph. Drake, who had been named as the murdered boy, was one of his older brothers.

Otherwise, most of the other facts in the case were correct and the piece on the 18th recapitulated the story, before going on to propose a motive for the brutal slaying. The paper reported that there had been a number of minor thefts at the camp in recent weeks. It speculated that young Ralph Andosca knew the identity of the thief and had been killed to prevent him from informing the authorities.

I know what some of you are thinking—the *Record* corrected one error only to make another.

You'd be right. The paper's hypothesis was fatally flawed. A few things had gone missing, but most of them had turned up found. If there had been a murderous thief among the construction crew, where would he have procured—and then cleverly hidden—the murder weapon? How could he have absented himself without his absence being noted by others in his crew? Would anyone really kill a child just to conceal a minor theft? Other than the men's wages, there was very little of monetary value in the camp, and none of the supposed thefts had involved money.

As a news item, the shooting disappeared from the paper until early the following week when the *Sherbrooke Daily Record* announced that two men had been apprehended and taken in for questioning. After Ayette and St. Pierre were released, the Melbourne Murder disappeared from the pages of the newspaper.

For a very brief few days the killing had been newsworthy. Inherently sensational—young boy murdered in cold blood!— it had been splashed as a news item quite far and wide, both in Canada and in the United States. The *Knickerbocker News*, published in Albany, the city nearest Ralph Andosca's home town, had given the story almost as much play as the *Sherbrooke Daily Record*. It was also the only paper that published more than one article on the murder; a second short piece appearing following the well-attended funeral of Ralph Andosca in his home town of Troy.

So, there you have it: a full description of the event, the investigation, and the enduring mystery of why twelve-year-old Ralph Andosca was shot in the back at close range with a shotgun and killed late on an otherwise unremarkable afternoon in the middle of August in 1905 in the bucolic setting of Melbourne Township.

Chapter 19

The missing piece of this puzzle, the reason Ralph Andosca was killed—or at least an account of other, parallel events leading up to the date of his murder—is in this diary. As you look at it, you can see that it's still an attractive volume; you can tell by the feel of it, and by its binding, that this was an expensive item in its day. How it came to be in the archives is an interesting story of its own, and I'll get back to that story in a minute. But first, since we now have the screen back, let's see what this diary reveals.

There's the screen!

As you can see, the flyleaf has been torn out. A detective might point out that it was probably torn out angrily. The most professional way to remove the flyleaf, or any other page, from a book is with a razor blade or a utility knife, or some other very sharp blade. With a sharp blade, the cut is so neat that unless you know the page was there, it's practically impossible to see that it's gone. It hasn't happened to us at the archives, at least as far as I know, but major libraries and museums have had priceless volumes vandalized by thieves who had black-market buyers willing to pay considerable sums for maps or illustrations from rare volumes dating back as far as the Middle Ages. The missing flyleaf in this diary, as you can see, has left a very ragged, saw-toothed remnant.

As we open the diary, we notice that the handwriting is very neat, very feminine. Our young diarist was probably using a fountain pen with a fine nib because the cursive script is almost like copperplate with those occasional curlicues and flourishes. Some of her capital letters have all the elegance of studied calligraphy, almost artwork. Attractive as the writing is, I imagine that for some of us, it is also a little tiring to read, in part because we're not quite used to it. As well, you can see that the ink has faded a little, but unevenly so that some of the letters are quite bold, while others appear faint.

Tuesday, 4:20

I am decided to accept my fate, simply awful as it is. I am still furious with Mater, even more so now that I have met these distant cousins and find myself in this ugly room that feels entirely as a prison cell. I do not at all want to think of this place as a home away from home, as it has been suggested I do. It is a vile little villa in the absolute middle of nowhere, yet how "Cousin John" and "Cousin Shirley" exult over it! They are both singularly loathsome people. It's an embarrassment that they are in some way related to Mater. I refuse to consider them as being related to me. I have only just met them and am already anxious to never see them again.

I am certainly not going to be going downstairs to join these supposed cousins for their evening meal. No doubt someone will knock at my door soon enough and I shall say that the trip here has exhausted me and that I want only to rest.

In truth, it is not at all true that the trip was particularly tiring. It actually seemed like a rather short ride to this backwoods outpost. Wilson put me on an Express that made only two short stops before I found myself disembarking at the Richmond station to transfer trains. I spent the entire first part of my trip tabulating a list of the varied ways that I intend to "innocently" or "inadvertently" make life as hellishly difficult (No! I do not excuse my language!) as I can for Mater and Jack when I am back home. I shall never forgive Mater for sending me off to this miserable hovel in this God-forsaken hamlet in the middle of the bush.

I certainly could have remained at home on my own, contrary to what Mater says. Furthermore, I would not have been alone. The servants are always there after all!

Instead Wilson brought me to the station against my will and forced me onto the train. To add to the humiliation, he kept my ticket from me and gave it directly to the conductor, whom he further instructed to surveil me. As the conductor quit my cabin, I am almost sure I saw Wilson slip money to him. When he turned back to me to hand me an envelope Wilson told me, in that syrupy voice I mistrust, "Your mother asked me to give you your allowance and she wants you to know that she's doubled it so that you can have an enjoyable vacation."

I have thought of ways to get my revenge on Wilson as well.

Nevertheless, the last part of my trip really was short, and it was genuinely pretty along the river.

When I disembarked, I immediately regretted that the ride hadn't been longer, or better yet that I had simply stayed on the train. But the idea didn't occur to me soon enough, and furthermore, the conductor, who smiled at me in a very unfriendly manner, came to my cabin to fetch me to make sure I did get off at my stop.

Perhaps he had that evil smile because he knew what was awaiting me.

I don't know how he recognized me but hardly a moment after I stepped off the train, out of nowhere came the horrid man I am to call "Cousin John."

Until two nights last, when Mater told me that I would not be travelling with her and Jack (whom I am henceforth to call Father although that is something I shall never do) I did not even know that such a creature as "Cousin John" even existed, leave alone that I had the misfortune of somehow being related to him, or rather that Mater is related to him, for I refuse to be. There was this horribly vile man rushing towards me with his arms outstretched and calling my name. Before I could stop him, he had taken me by the shoulders and given me a peck on each cheek. It was all I could do not to wipe my face with my gloved hand, and if I had not been holding my two suitcases I would have.

"Here, Cousin, let me take these from you, and let me introduce you to your Cousin Shirley."

My "Cousin Shirley," who was suddenly bearing down on me, looked even more odious than her husband. She is a big-bosomed woman who looked like nothing so much as a Spanish galleon under full sail with billowing canvas dwarfing an all but invisible undercarriage. She was so garishly dressed that I didn't at first notice her face. I shall describe it simply by saying that it could stop a clock. Her eyes are hidden behind spectacles that might have been fashionable half a century ago. Her glasses totter precariously on her long, narrow nose. It's as well that she wears spectacles because her eyes are set wide apart and give her the look of someone who is either momentarily dumbfounded or congenitally cretinous. I should also mention that she has bad skin that is not at all hidden by all her powder and rouge, and as if that were not enough, she had obviously doused herself far too liberally with the most offensive perfume that I have ever encountered. It's a wonder I didn't keel over when she too gave me a peck on each cheek.

Compared to his unpardonably ugly wife, Cousin John could almost pass for a tolerably handsome man with his regular features and prematurely white hair. However, his face is positively florid, as if his shirt collar is too tight and all his blood has been trapped above his neck.

He is a man with the pompous mannerisms of a proud peacock. For example, he made a great show of taking his cheap, silver-plated watch from his fob pocket and flipping it open to announce that we should be on our way. He said that he had to get back to his store where we would make a brief stop so that I could meet their son.

"I'm sure you will adore Dixon-Albert," Shirley squeaked, suggesting that I should somehow join in her enthusiasm.

"You'll get along famously," she assured me and went on to tell me how wonderful this son of theirs is. "He's only nineteen, you know, and although he is still in training, he is already one of the very best clerks in the store. He's a very bright boy, you know. He has his junior matriculation. We wanted him to go on to get his senior matriculation but he so enjoys working in the store that we couldn't say no to him."

I could have pointed out to the fat cow that getting one's junior matriculation at nineteen is hardly an indication of a superior intellect. The fact is that anyone who is the least bit capable will obtain it by the simple expedience of staying awake in class and do so years before one's nineteenth birthday. (Certainly I intend to have my junior matriculation the year after next, although as Miss Nott has told me more than once, it seems that I am somewhat precocious.)

The store that "Cousin John" is so proud of turned out to be a vulgar affair. When we entered a bell above the door clanged as if it had been hit with a sledgehammer. The floor was scuffed and liberally sprinkled with sawdust, at least on the customers' side of the long counter where half a dozen men stood while being served by half that number of sales clerks.

"Cousin John" led us to the back of the store where two clerks, ensconced in small cubicles, were working assiduously at their desks. He led us up a short flight of steps and into a relatively spacious windowed office that overlooked the store.

Presently, one of the clerks disengaged himself and a moment later entered the office and I was in the exalted presence of Dixon-Albert, of whom I had already heard far too much. Unsurprisingly, given his parentage, he looked as stupid as his absurd hyphenated name sounded. Physically, he looks something like a cross between a mule and medium-sized bear. He has a long face marred by prominent upper teeth that seem to hang much too far over his lower jaw. He has pale eyes that seemed incapable of remaining focussed on anyone or anything, but were continually darting all over the room, as if he were surreptitiously looking for a hatch through which he might escape. Like his mother, he has bad skin, in his case, sprinkled more generously than necessary with horrid little yellow pimples across his forehead. He has his mother's solid build, a body not yet turned to portly fat but already with a few layers more lard than necessary. When his garrulous mother introduced him, he half stuttered and half muttered a greeting of some kind. Thank God that he didn't try to give me a peck on the cheek as his besotted parents did. I didn't have so much as a single suitcase with which to protect myself, not that I'd been able to use them to save myself at the train station. (Nanny packed them so heavily that it was all I could do to lift them off the ground; even with two hands I doubt I could lift even one to shoulder height.)

There was a deliciously awkward moment when "Cousin John" announced that he had to stay at the store and suggested that "Cousin Shirley" should drive us home. "Cousin Shirley," acting the Grand Lady, pointedly told her husband, "But you know I can't drive the carriage!" and "Cousin John" had to call one of his employees from the lumberyard to drive us home.

It was a thankfully short ride, and fortunately there was enough of a breeze to blow away the nauseating fumes of Cousin Shirley's perfume, at least most of the time.

We were driven a short distance along the Main Street before turning at a crossroads that led us immediately to a covered bridge that spanned the St. Francis. I was ever so grateful to the bridge for its echo. The sound of the horse's hooves and the carriage's steel-rimmed wheels echoed loudly and caused an infernal racket that made it impossible to hear. Even "Cousin Shirley," whom

I have concluded is as dim-witted as she is ugly, realized that it was best to simply remain quiet. Up until this point she had kept up an unrelenting barrage of questions (that I answered with monosyllables or not at all) and commentary (that ranged from totally irrelevant to utterly inane). The echoing clatter of hooves and wheels over the bridge's wooden boards was almost musical by comparison. Unfortunately, the confines of the covered bridge compounded the noxious fumes of her perfume.

Immediately over the bridge we came to another crossroads and we turned downstream, the direction from which we had come, and passed by half a dozen dwellings which ranged from cabins to shacks to hovels before we came to a modestly pretentious, brick-clad house where the carriage stopped and garrulous "Cousin Shirley" exclaimed, "We're home!"

She immediately embarked upon a tour of the premises, determined to show me every nook and cranny, every closet and curtain rod.

I feigned exhaustion and asked to only be shown to my room that I might rest. The only other place I would need to know the location of was the water closet.

The house, for all of its cunningly modern, pride-inducing architectural brilliance, does not have indoor plumbing, other than a hand pump that brings water from a well into the kitchen sink. (That water is used for washing but not for drinking; the potable water is fetched at a nearby spring, and a pitcher of cold water can always be found in the ice box.) Thus, there is no WC in this pseudo-stupendous domicile, rather, "Cousin Shirley" told me, there is a chamber pot in my room, under the bed. Of course, she added, I could also use what she called the "privy" at the end of the garden, which is not a garden at all but a riot of weeds running rampant through what may once have been vegetable beds.

My room, which had been made to sound sumptuous and grand as we trod up the stairs, turned out to be small and cramped.

Were it to be measured, the room would possibly be the size of my dressing room at home. It does have a window (unlike my dressing room at home) and it faces east, overlooking the garden, a small carriage house, the privy, and beyond that, the river. I can already see myself sitting all day at the window keeping track of the trains that run along the opposite bank. One is chugging upstream this very moment. If I have time between trains, I could keep track of how often one or another of the family treks out to the privy!

There is no dressing room but only a closet in which to hang my dresses, of which Nanny, I am sure, packed too many.

After I unpack—something I insisted on doing myself entirely without any of the help that "Cousin Shirley" kept offering—I shall have to put the suitcases somewhere and I think it will have to be with the chamber pot under the bed. Really! A chamber pot is just the touch to make one feel that one has stepped back in time into the last century!

"Cousin Shirley" made a point of telling me, more than once, that the municipal government will soon be laying pipes under the front roadway that will provide both water and drainage facilities to all of the houses on the River Road. When this house was erected only four years ago, she went on, the builders made provisions and left room for a bathroom and a WC.

The bed is smaller than what I have at home, but at least better than the camp cot I had to sleep on for two weeks last summer.

It would not do to be overly negative so I will say that I find no fault with the small desk and chair, which I am currently putting to use.

The room is papered, rather garishly as one might have expected given Cousin Shirley's atrocious attire. The most attractive feature of the room is the floor which is of polished wood and quite lustrous. Beside the bed is a small rug so placed that I need not step onto a cold surface when I arise in the morning, although, given that we're in August I can't imagine the floor will be particularly cold during my stay which I pray will be brief. I have no intention of being here any longer than I have to, certainly not till the arrival of winter, or even fall. How long can Mater and Jack be away?

Still, I am here, and I suppose I shall have to accept it.

There are my suitcases. I will have to unpack them, but really, I have no energy for it right now. I shall let them be for the time being. But I will lie down. The recounting of the afternoon, I believe, has left me tired, or depressed. I can't tell which.

Chapter 20

I'm going to stop there for just a minute because I am sure that you have a lot of questions, just as I had when I first read this.

There, the screen is off.

Yes! A lot of questions: Who wrote this diary? How did it come to find itself in our archives? What can it possibly have to do with the murder of young Ralph Andosca?

We don't have an answer to the first question, which is perhaps not so very surprising. A diary is a highly personal document, written only for oneself. The writer—diarist I should probably say—may reveal all manner of inner torment and turmoil, especially if the diarist in question is an adolescent, but it is unlikely that he or she will reveal his or her name. It is possible that if we had the missing flyleaf, we might have had that name. It's easy to imagine that "Mater" (whoever she was) gave the diary (a very attractive item that would have been a very nice gift) to her daughter and inscribed something on the flyleaf: 'To my daughter Jane,' or 'To Mary for her daily journal,' something along those lines that might have given us at least a first name.

But the flyleaf is gone and so the diarist's name remains unknown.

However, we do know who John, and Shirley, and Dixon-Albert were, thanks to the references to a hardware store in Windsor and to a relatively recently built house in Greenlay. This was the Spicker family. All three are listed in the census of

1901 and 1911 as being domiciled on the River Road in Greenlay. John and Shirley continued to live there at least until 1931. The house they had built, unfortunately, was heavily damaged by fire in 1982 and was subsequently demolished. The lot was subdivided, and an enterprising contractor put up a couple of bungalows in its place.

Such is our architectural history.

Spicker we know to have been a relatively prosperous merchant who was quite active in his community. He was a member of the local Masonic lodge, and the St. Andrew's Society, which were, to one extent or another, benevolent societies that provided the social safety nets that welfare and medicare provide us with today. Early in the twentieth century, he served one term as alderman in Greenlay.

We can only wonder who his young cousin might have been, and how she came to leave her diary behind.

The diary, as you can see, is an attractive, leather-bound book that's about three centimetres thick and measures about twenty centimetres by fourteen centimetres.

It came to the Society from Belinda Clarke, whose name some of you no doubt remember. She operated Melbourne's library for over half a century, and only stopped in 1999 when the town amalgamated with Richmond and people on the Melbourne side of the river acquired access to the municipal library on the Richmond side of the river. Mrs. Clarke's library, which she herself referred to as the Melbourne Library, was not a municipal service, but was her own private enterprise. (Although, I've been told, her property taxes were adjusted to reflect her ongoing contribution to the municipality.)

When amalgamation came, many thought that she would be devastated by the loss of her library. She was not a young woman, and it was a commonly held belief that it was the library that was keeping her as spry as she was.

To everyone's relief, she was glad to see her books passed on to someone else to look after.

Belinda Clark was born in 1919. She had taken over as the library's custodian—and she thought of it in those terms, as having custody of the books as someone might have custody of an orphan child—in 1941.

Prior to that, the library had been in the care of Florence Underwood, whose distant ancestor, Elliston Underwood was one of the area's earliest settlers and, along with Squire Daniel Thomas, a founding member of the Craig Union Library that was created here in 1815. That first library had no bricks or mortar; it was a collection of books available on loan that were kept by one or another of the library trustees. Florence Underwood was carrying on that tradition.

Florence Underwood, who was Belinda Clarke's spinster aunt, died suddenly in the winter of 1941 after suffering a sudden stroke. Belinda moved into her aunt's home, where the library was housed, and continued her aunt's work.

The same day that she moved into her aunt's house, she learned that her husband, Anthony Clarke, a corporal in the Canadian army had been killed in an accident on a training base in Nova Scotia. She had been married to him for less than three months.

Deprived of a future with the man she had expected would share the house that she had so fortuitously come to own, the Melbourne Lending Library became her life. It took up two adjoining rooms: the parlour and dining room of her aunt's Victorian-style, brick-clad house. Even though the two rooms together had little more than five hundred square feet of floor space, there was shelving on every square foot of available wall surface, enough for almost fifteen hundred volumes. The place was a little cramped; a small desk, a filing cabinet and two chest-high bookcases were squeezed into the rooms, but everything was always very tidy and orderly. Until the last few years, Belinda kept her collection surprisingly up-to-date. She would order books that her clients requested, and she kept as many English titles on her shelves as French. She periodically culled her shelves and refreshed her titles. From time to time, she would hold a book sale, but some of the books that she culled from the library shelves she kept for herself elsewhere in the house. A client who asked about a novel he'd read a quarter century before was often pleased when Belinda would say, "I think I still have it," and reappear a few minutes later with the book in question. She was not shy about charging a pretty penny for special requests of this nature; in her own way, she was an astute businesswoman. Aside from the three small rooms that were her living quarters, the rest of her house served to store books.

Belinda ran the library in a businesslike manner. She opened at regular hours, including two evenings a week until eight o'clock, and Saturday mornings. She was punctual about annual library card renewals, and she was strict about overdue books. Still, the library was more a vocation than it was a business enterprise. With only a few hundred clients the library provided her with only a meagre income. She was able to get by because she received a small war widow's pension, and she was the beneficiary of her aunt's will. She lived simply, if not frugally. She didn't drive. She walked to the Post Office and across the bridge to the grocery store, and on Sundays she walked in the other direction, right here, to the Presbyterian Church, even though, especially in her later years, that represented a bit of a hike for her.

After amalgamation, with her library closed, Belinda sold the house and moved into the Wales Home. Not all of her collection went to the municipal library. She packed two boxes, each with some two dozen books—most on local or Eastern

Townships history, and long since removed from her own shelves—and made a donation of them to the Historical Society. The diary was in one of those boxes.

As often happens to books put into boxes, they stayed in their boxes for some time before even a first attempt was made to catalogue them. This diary, along with a few other items in one of the boxes, didn't come up for cataloguing until this summer. If she were still with us, Belinda Clarke might have been able to tell us more about this diary: how it came to be in her possession, and perhaps even whose it was. But she passed away almost a decade ago.

She was, in some ways, quite a remarkable woman. She suffered a deep personal loss and somehow transformed it into a life-long service to her community. She remained healthy and lucid until the last few days before she died.

The diary came to my attention after it was "discovered" while the exhibit *Consequential Women / Femmes Incontournables* was being mounted. Belinda Clarke was chosen as one of the two dozen local women from the nineteenth and twentieth centuries to be singled out for their contributions to Richmond and the surrounding area. Those of you who saw the exhibit remember how it was set up. There was a photo of the woman being honoured, a brief biographical note, and a few items that reflected her particular contribution to the community.

It was one of our summer students, Janice Giguère, who ended up stumbling across the forgotten box of books from Belinda. Because the diary had such a nice cover, and since it had a direct link to Belinda and her library, it was used as part of Belinda's display.

It wasn't until later on in the summer that anyone actually took a look at the diary, and that happened thanks to a visitor, and again to Janice who was giving a brief tour of our museum and the *Consequential Women* exhibit.

"What a lovely binding," the visitor said. "And it's a diary! Is it as interesting as its cover?"

Janice had replied, "I don't know. I've never read it."

"Isn't that a shame," even though the woman had smiled politely as she said this, Janice felt that she had fallen short in her duty as a museum guide.

It was when Janice came to me with this story that I realized that the diary, like a number of the other books in the box it had been found in, had never been catalogued. Janice seemed quite interested to read the diary, and it had to be at least perused to catalogue it, so I told her that between visitors and the other odd jobs she had to do, she could read the diary as part of her job description. I could then quiz her on it and that might be enough to catalogue it.

Of course, at a certain point, I realized that I had to read it myself.

And now that you know a little more about its provenance, I'm sure you'd like to read a little more of the diary for yourselves.

OK! The screen is still working.

Chapter 21

A knock at my door startled me out of my slumber and for a moment I could make no sense of my surroundings. I had somehow fallen asleep even though I had had no intention of doing more than resting for a minute before undertaking the task of emptying my two suitcases.

"Excuse me, Miss," said the maid who pushed my door open and peeked her head around it. "Mrs. Spicker says to let you know to come down to the dining room for supper."

"I shan't be eating," I told her.

"Are you sure, Miss? Although it's fine if you don't. I'll tell Mrs. Spicker," she said and withdrew.

But she was back again two minutes later, "Mrs. Spicker is asking if you're unwell. Would you need anything at all? She said she'd be up to see you immediately after they've dined."

"I'm fine," I told her. "After my trip, I'm not hungry. That's all. There's no need for her to come see me. I shall be resting and don't want to be disturbed."

Of course, the next time there was a knock at my door it was "Cousin Shirley" who came barging in like a buffalo. It took forever to get her out of my room. Was I certain that I was well? Did I have travelling sickness? Was I homesick? Did I want a bowl of chicken soup to settle my stomach? Or a glass of milk? Did I want help unpacking my suitcases? Would I be able to sleep well in a new bed? Did I want a glass of cold water? Would I remember that the water in the ewer was just for washing? The drinking water was kept cold in a pitcher in the ice box. Was I sure that I didn't need anything at all? Perhaps a cup of warm cacao? Was I sure I didn't want help unpacking? Was I too tired to come downstairs for a minute to bid good night to Cousin John and Dixon-Albert?

Now that she's finally gone I realize that I won't be able to simply remain in my room for the duration of my stay, as I was thinking of doing, not unless I want to have "Cousin Shirley" storming in here to put me through that kind of interrogation on a daily basis, if not hourly. It is too easy to imagine her crashing through the door a dozen times a day. I shall have to think of something.

I am, in fact, feeling rather peckish just now. But I'll be damned if I go downstairs! (Yes, damned, and I mean damned!)

...

I've just been saved by the maid. I had started unpacking my suitcases, and in fact had one almost completely unpacked when she again knocked at the door to bring me a glass of cold water.

"In case you need a sip of water during the night," she said.

"Thank you."

"Will there be anything else, Miss?"

I was about to say no, but before I could say a word, my stomach made itself heard, in a most unladylike manner.

"You didn't eat this evening, Miss. Would you like me to get you something? I could make a sandwich for you, if you wish."

"Yes, please, I am feeling a little hungry just now."

"There's some ham in the icebox, if you like ham, Miss."

I don't much care for ham and I started to say so, but at that moment, I didn't much care what I ate. As well, there was something about her that made me not want to burden the maid further. (If it had been Wilson, I'd have asked for a dish that would take him forever to prepare! Something like asparagus-stuffed crepes drizzled with a béchamel sauce.)

"That would be fine," I told her, and something made me add, "and you needn't hurry on my account."

She didn't hurry perhaps, but nevertheless she was at the door with a sandwich and a glass of milk only a short while later.

"If you would leave the plate and glass just outside your door, Miss, I can fetch them without disturbing. Good night, Miss."

As it happened, I did not immediately eat but finished emptying the essentials from my suitcases, sorted, folded, and hung my own clothes (just like camp last year!), and only then did I eat my sandwich, so that the sun was already setting and dusk was falling by the time I opened my door to leave my plate and empty glass on the hall floor.

The maid just happened to be coming up the stairs at the same time and I was glad of that because it was growing dark and I had just noticed that there was no electricity in this house but that there was an oil lamp on a small corner shelf. I had no idea how to light it, so it was rather fortuitous that the maid should have presented herself just then.

It took her a minute to adjust the wick, strike a match, replace the glass and provide light for the room, or at least enough light to continue writing or to read. She showed me how to adjust it for brightness and how to extinguish the flame.

It was as she was doing so that I noticed that the maid is not as old as I had first thought. When I first set eyes on her, I thought her to be a woman of five and twenty, but I'm quite sure now that she's much younger. Perhaps I shall ask her.

There is something that strikes me as unusual about her although I can't quite say what it is. Being younger than what she at first seemed is just part of her unusualness, I'm sure of that. On the one hand she looks faintly mournful, as if she's burdened by a deep sorrow, but yet she seems to carry an aura of hidden strength, of a fierce will to survive.

As I now think of it, she must have enormous endurance to put up with "Cousin Shirley." I think if I were in her shoes I would leave; indeed, I would never have taken employment in this house in the first place. Servants may not be able to choose for whom they work, but they can surely choose for whom not to work.

That's another puzzle. Why ever would she choose to work here? Surely, to be a servant to "Cousin Shirley" is a fate worse than death. I shall have to find a way to discover that. Why would a young woman—perhaps only a girl not that much older than I—who is quite competent in her work, polite in her manners, and blessed with regular features want to work for a woman as perfectly odious as the mistress of this house?

Chapter 22

I'm interrupting just for a minute to tell you that we're going to skip ahead a bit here. Our young diarist was a very enthusiastic scribe and a prolific writer. The passages you've just read were all written by her on her first day in Greenlay, and she only arrived late in the afternoon. If we were to read the entire diary we'd be here till midnight. Not that it isn't interesting reading.

The diary grows more interesting as it grows more relevant to the murder of Ralph Andosca. From the very beginning, we know that the diarist was living—at least temporarily—very near the site of the murder. In three different passages that come a little later on we learn that she was there in August of 1905. Even though she only ever indicates the day of the week, if that, and not the date, in two separate entries she makes reference to events that place these diary entries at the time just before Ralph Andosca was murdered.

Wednesday

At breakfast CS announced that we would go to Richmond as she had some shopping to do.

"We'll make a day of it, Dear! There are some lovely shops on Main Street that I just know you will adore! I must stop at the milliner, and at the pharmacy—I don't like the pharmacist here in Windsor so I always use Mr. Hebert in Richmond; his staff are ever so courteous and helpful—and we'll stop at the Post Office as well, as I need stamps. I'm sure you'll need a stamp as well, won't you, Dear, for your letter to your Mother. But you needn't bother, as I'm buying a whole sheet, and I'm glad to give you a stamp for your letter to your Mother. But there are so many shops! Well, perhaps not many from your point of comparison, I know, but really there are several lovely ones, and we can just window shop, but we can visit any shop you wish."

I didn't wish to visit any shop at all, but that was no deterrent to CS. We disembarked at the Richmond station and set out on our shopping trip. We walked to the very end of Main Street, or at least until there were no more shops for CS to burst into; then we turned around and walked all the way back to the train station. I would not have minded the walk were it not for the company and were it not for the fact that we only ever walked a few dozen paces before we again had to stop to stare into a shop window or knock down a shop door. We didn't walk so much as stand about.

Fortunately Richmond's Main Street was actually not so terribly long, not in actual distance. We were lucky as well with the weather. It remained clear and quite sunny for almost the duration of our excursion. We were just opening the doors of the Brunswick Hotel when the sky, which had quite suddenly turned dark, opened up and a torrential rain started falling.

We had quite a nice lunch in the dining room of the Brunswick Hotel, and when we stepped back outside, there were puddles on the ground, but the sky was a brilliant blue and perfectly cloudless. The station was directly across the street and we had to wait some time for the train. The boarding platform is quite long at the Richmond station and I would have been quite happy to stroll it just for the pleasure of moving. CS wanted only to sit.

With the excuse of going to procure a copy of a newspaper to read I was able to stroll the platform several times and CS was able to doze peacefully in the shade. At least until an incoming engine announced its arrival. Poor CS was so startled at the sound of its whistle that she bounced off the bench as if she were a jack-in-the-box.

I quite enjoyed the short ride to Windsor, just as I had before, or almost as much because CS had been reanimated by her nap and talked almost incessantly.

Did I know that they're building a railroad to Greenlay? Did I know that the station will be built just a little way along the road from their home? Was I not scandalized that it was Italians building it? But was I not grateful that, at least, you never saw them, and they stayed on their construction site? Did I not feel much safer that way? I did know that they were all criminals and thieves, did I not? And that I must never speak to an Italian?

The most remarkable thing about CS is that the most unremarkable thing can set her off in the most unexpected directions. Her venomous, vituperative tirade began when she noticed a plume of smoke rising from the forest on the other side of the river.

There were a number of buggies and wagons lined up near the station, but Cousin John's was not among them and we had to walk to Cousin John's store and wait for one of the men in the lumberyard to hitch the buggy to drive us home which gave CS plenty of time to berate Cousin John for having forgotten that we were coming back on the afternoon train and should it not have been at the station waiting for us?

What was waiting for CS at home was a horse and wagon, although it was not actually waiting for her so much as taking advantage of her absence. Nor was it waiting quite where it should have been.

The Spicker monstrosity sits further back from the road than the other half-dozen or so properties that line it a little haphazardly. There are no sidewalks, of course, so one steps out of one's castle and onto the road, although in CS's case, house and road are separated by several yards of front garden. The property is delineated by a border of flower beds. They are two or three feet wide and run the full length of the front yard, except for the openings for the laneway that leads to the carriage house and the walk that leads to the front door—a door that is almost never used. CS's flower beds line one side of the lane and both sides of the front walk as well as the frontage along the road.

As we arrived at the house, we noticed a horse and wagon although not where they might have been expected to be on the side of the road, but rather half onto the front yard, straddling the flower bed, part way along to the front walk.

Pierre, the man from the lumberyard, had us alight from the buggy at the mouth of the laneway, niftily turned the buggy around, and was out of sight by the time that CS was fully cognizant of the fact that the horse, still harnessed to the wagon, was contentedly masticating on the colour and verdure of the flowerbeds!

"No!" she yelled. "My hostas!"

She shoved her bags and boxes at me and ran to do battle with the sweet-tooth steed. She ran at the animal in full voice, slapped at its neck, and tugged at the bridle reins and succeeded only in making it momentarily lift its head with a quizzical look at its assailant.

When I stepped through the kitchen door, I found Colleen at the kitchen sink and, at the kitchen table, a young man who startled as I walked in.

He immediately sprang to his feet and dove for the door. Over his shoulder he called, "Thank you muchly for the glass of water," and he was gone. He was back half a second later to pick up a battered green felt hat from the back of the chair on which he'd been sitting, and again disappeared.

It was several minutes before CS came into the house, still fuming. Samuel Brightwood, the young man who had left the kitchen with such alacrity, had apparently come to deliver eggs. However long can it take Samuel Brightwood to deliver two dozen eggs, given that the man's horse had cropped almost half of CS's flower beds? Water? The man asked for a glass of water when the spring is but a few dozen yards down the road? Whyever would he need a glass of water from this house with the spring almost across the road? And what need was there for the man to come into the kitchen? Could he not have delivered the eggs to the door without ever coming in? And how long can it take a man to drink a glass of water? Surely a man should be able to drink a glass of water in less time than it takes a horse to eat a yardful of flowers? Was it understood that the Brightwood man would never again step into this house? Whyever did Colleen allow him to stay as long as he did?

"He said he wanted to speak to you, Ma'am, and I expected you'd be back any minute."

"Speak to me!" CS sputtered and stuttered and began to turn purple with apoplexy.

If Brightwood really had wanted to speak to CS I imagine he didn't get much of a chance. Once CS starts up it's more than difficult to get her stopped, even when she's not livid with rage. It was actually quite amusing to see how Colleen did shut her up, although I'm not at all sure that Brightwood actually had an interest in speaking to CS.

I expect it was Colleen he wanted to speak with. When he arrived and found CS out of the house, he no doubt spoke to her much longer than he expected he would, long enough in any case that he quite forgot about his horse at the mouth of the laneway.

I suppose I should feel a little bit of empathy for poor old CS. Her flowerbeds were not unattractive, not that I could tell a petunia from a pansy, but if you are to have a riot of uncontrolled colours, better in a flowerbed than in a wardrobe.

Chapter 23

This next entry appears a few days later:

4:00

The day has again been barometrically brutal with sun and cloud playing tag since this morning. CS, of course, fluctuates even more wildly than the weather; she is smiling blissfully one minute and then scowling angrily the next. As I've noted before, it takes nothing at all to set her off, and it's clear that Colleen is like a human lightning rod for CS's tempestuous tantrums. It happened again this afternoon.

This morning, while it was pleasant and sunny, CS called me to do my daily needlepoint, which I endured for half an hour or so before my delicate wrist began ailing me to the point that I really could not manage another stitch. I make sure to vary my maladies: my eyes, my fingers, my back, my shoulder, my buttocks have all pained me most dreadfully; and some days, just to confuse my dear Cousin Shirley, I make not a single complaint and even convey a touch of disappointment that we have to stop this most enjoyable and most ladylike pastime so soon. Of course, I do this on those mornings that, because of some household crisis, or routine chore, or other distraction, CS is unable to collar me for my dose of needlepoint until late in the ante meridiem.

But this morning, I complained of my wrist and CS showed hardly any displeasure at all. In fact, she seemed glad to go out to counsel (or more likely confuse) the man who'd come to salvage the flower beds. Of course, ten minutes after she stepped out the door, the sky clouded over.

I had intended to take a postprandial promenade but of course I had to wait for Colleen (for a young lady—a category of creature to which I have the misfortune of belonging—cannot walk unaccompanied) and by the time Colleen had got all of her work done and was free to go, the sky had clouded over again and I thought better of it. It was just as well for shortly after there was a tremendous thunder burst and for a few minutes the rain was torrential. The downpour died out just as quickly as it had started but of course it left the road slick with mud and pockmarked with puddles. I no longer wished to walk as I was quite immersed in my reading just then.

As it happened, after lunch, I installed myself in my favourite chair in the front parlour (where CS insisted I should read—rather than in the privacy of my room which I still prefer) and sat down with Penelope Farthing's most recent book. I imagine CS would be absolutely scandalized were she to learn that I am reading a crime novel that involves a murder. Penelope Farthing is quite the rage right now and it seems that everyone is reading her, and I am determined to do so as well, at least so that I might know what all the fuss is about. I've only just begun the book, but it is quite a compelling read so far.

Still, fascinating as the fiction was, I had to put the book down just after Colleen returned from fetching water at the spring because a moment after she came in, CS descended on her like a cloudburst and it was impossible to not overhear her.

What happened seemed innocent enough to me. Not long after three o'clock, after the thunder burst and after the skies had cleared, Colleen left the house to fetch potable water from the spring as she does at least once every day. I have no idea how long she was gone, but I do know that by the time she returned it was drizzling again. The parlour door had been left open so that I heard the kitchen door close behind Colleen when she came back in. And then I heard CS stomping down the stairs, storming into the kitchen, and lashing into Colleen.

Where had she been all this time? Why had it taken so long for her to fetch an ewer of water? Had she again been gadding about at the spring? CS had heard from Mrs. Heriot that she had been seen talking to a young man, and now CS wanted to know was it the same young man from whose wagon she had just disembarked? Did she not know that she had no business climbing onto a stranger's wagon? Was she no longer capable of walking one hundred yards back from the spring just because of a little rain? It had better not happen again, that was all CS was going to say about it. This was a respectable home and CS was going to ensure that it remained that way. CS certainly hoped that she wouldn't be getting any more reports from Mrs. Heriot. And CS certainly hoped that the young man on the wagon wasn't from that crew of criminals who were constructing the rail line! They were all thieving, murderous Italians and no one in a respectable household like the Spickers will have anything to do with them. They are to absolutely be avoided like the plague.

Unfortunately, I somehow dropped Penelope Farthing just then and I had to pretend that I was on my way upstairs to my room to rest before supper, and not lurking by the door to better listen in on CS's tirade.

Although if it spared Colleen an even longer tongue lashing, I am glad, and I wish I had made a noise the moment CS started in on her.

I shall have to keep my eyes and ears open. If there is something going on, I am curious to know what it is.

In the meantime, I will read a few more pages of Miss Farthing's opus while I wait for the call to supper.

Chapter 24

We're going to skip ahead again. In this next passage our diarist gets an answer to the question she had asked herself at the end of her first day with the redoubtable Cousin Shirley: why was the maid working for her?

Saturday, 4:30

We are just back from a place pretentiously called Coney Island. The last three days CS has done nothing but talk about Coney Island. How wonderful it was! How perfectly lovely it was! How popular it was with all the smart people from as far away as Sherbrooke! How I would simply adore the place! And how marvellous it was that we were going all four! (Cousin John and Dixon-Albert work only a half day on Saturday, CS told me almost conspiratorially; their commerce closes at noon liberating them to spend the afternoon together with us.) How I would have something special about which to write to my mother.

By my mother, CS means Mater.

I haven't of course written a word to Mater. Nor shall I.

I've noticed that this is putting CS in a bit of a dither. CS has not said so yet, not in so many words, but she is quite nervous that I've not yet replied to Mater's postcard that arrived two days past. A proper young lady, one with manners, really would have replied immediately, even if it were only a quick note to send off on the next post. If I did not reply the same day (one might receive mail too late to get to the Post Office before its closing at 6:00), CS expected I would write Mater the next morning, or at least the next day. That two days have passed, and I have not yet produced an envelope with Mater's name on it to be delivered to the Post Office has prompted CS to hint on two or three occasions that I must write Mater as soon as possible. I sense that CS is growing increasingly mortified that this "faux pas" is being committed under her roof, and what is worse, by someone of whom she is nominally in charge.

I wonder if CS will not raise the topic tomorrow. Tomorrow will be Sunday and I expect that tomorrow morning they will all be tripping over each other as they dress for Sunday Services. But I shouldn't be surprised if CS doesn't pull me aside at some point and tell me, "Don't you think, Dear, that you really should write to your mother? After all, it has been several days."

"No," I will tell her. "Several is a word meaning six or seven or perhaps more (though less than a dozen) so while it may feel that it's been an eternity since Mater's letter arrived, if one actually counts the days, it is not yet six."

Although, after today's debacle, I'm wondering if CS will still be anxious to have me write to "my mother" as she puts it. I'm quite sure that CS would absolutely not want me to describe this after-noon's outing to the less fabled Coney Island in a letter to Mater.

We left the house a little after 1:30. This was later than the time CS had planned. The fault lay with "Cousin John" who had been unable to close up his hardware store promptly at noon. Dixon-Albert arrived home with the message that his father hoped to be no more than ten minutes. In fact, the meal that was supposed to have been served at 12:15 was served at 12:55. I'm sure it would have been a perfectly comestible meal at 12:15 but by the time I picked up my knife and fork, the meat had grown dry and tough, the potatoes cold and crumbly, and the vegetables limp and soggy.

"Cousin John" made a point of berating Colleen for the meal but he did so when she was safely in the kitchen and conveniently out of hearing. No one bothered to reply to his comment, either in support or denial, and I imagine even he realized how false he was being, as the failed dinner was entirely his fault.

It was still sunny when we left but with a little wind and some clouds in the east. It was a pleasant enough ride along the River Road, and we didn't go very far, no more than half an hour at a steady trot. I had no idea that we'd arrived when Dixon-Albert pulled the buggy over behind a very long line of similarly parked wagons and carriages.

We disembarked and walked the rest of the way which must have taken us at least five minutes. By the time we crossed the long footbridge to the much-fabled Coney Island, the sun had disappeared and the air had grown cooler.

It didn't actually start to rain until we'd walked to the other end of the island (this did not take more than two minutes, I am sure) and purchased our ice cream cones (these too, CS had been extolling enthusiastically the last few days).

Quite suddenly it grew dark and the clouds seemed to descend as low as the treetops. At first, the rain was very light, a gentle rain of small drops that fell far apart. We waited with others under an awning, but within a few minutes the rain had changed to a heavier and steadier shower. For a moment the rain seemed it was going to let up but instead there came a tremendous downpour; the rain was streaming from the sky and bouncing huge droplets off the ground that started turning almost immediately into mud.

The downpour lasted several minutes but eventually let up and it eventually stopped altogether. For a moment there was great joy in Mudville. A spontaneous cheer went up from all when the sun broke through the clouds. A moment later, its warming rays caused faint, ephemeral wisps of steam to rise from almost everywhere because almost everything was soaking wet.

Even though we'd been sheltered by the awning of the ice cream stand, I had nevertheless managed, like everyone else, to get a little wet, and my feet of course were soaked through.

CS took heart from this sunburst and was ready to continue with her agenda, for she had a list of experiences to be had on Coney Island, and next on her schedule was a boat ride.

I'm quite sure both "Cousin John" and Dixon-Albert had their misgivings. Both looked tentatively more than once at a sky with any number of scurrying clouds. We had just pushed off from the quay when the rain started. This time there was nothing tentative or spectacular about it. It was a regular rain: unrelentingly steady, promising to stay so for several hours, and penetratingly, soakingly, drenchingly wet. The much-ballyhooed boat ride was as short as the trudge back to the buggy was long.

To add to the misery, Dixon-Albert managed to clip a marker with one of the buggy wheels. Fortunately, this happened on the very last stretch home. CS and I walked the last few hundred yards home in the mud while the men sorted out the problem with the wheel.

The image that I think I shall forever keep of poor old CS is the picture she presented as she stood at the kitchen door. She was a perfect wet hen.

Wet hen reminds me! The most surprising thing I learned today—this was at Coney Island, just as we were about to cross the footbridge leading to the island when we all stopped so that CS could exchange pleasantries (or gossip) with one of her numberless acquaintances—what I learned was that the maid that CS employs is neither a maid nor an employee.

CS keeps a home girl! It is an indentured servant who cooks and cleans for CS, not a maid who is given a stipend and is free to seek a less horrid employer! For CS is quite horrid with Colleen, and hyperbolically hypocritical about her at the same time. On the one hand she frequently berates her or prompts henpecked

"Cousin John" to upbraid her for a triviality, or for something not of her doing. Then, on the other hand, she's forever preening her own feathers, and lauds and praises Colleen's competence and efficiency—although never in Colleen's presence.

I have wondered since my arrival why Colleen would remain here with such odious creatures as the Spickers. The answer is simple: it is because she is a slave, enduring her period of penal servitude until her sentence has expired.

Colleen said something enigmatic a few days past, and I now understand what she meant. After she turns eighteen, at the end of the summer, her life will be her own. I can easily imagine that when CS tumbles out of bed the morning of Colleen's birthday she will not find the table set for breakfast nor hear the tea kettle whistling in the kitchen, for I would not be surprised that Colleen is planning to leave this domicile at the stroke of midnight of her eighteenth birthday.

Chapter 25

I'm going to interrupt just for another moment before we skip to the next passage in the diary. As you've just seen, our diarist has discovered that the Spicker's maid was a home child. I think all of us know at least a little about the home children. We know that for the better part of a century, children between the ages of four and fifteen were being shipped from England to different colonies and countries in the British Empire by the tens of thousands where they were quite often badly used as free labour. Their stories were usually sad, and sometimes tragic. Yet many survived, and a surprisingly large number of people in this country now proudly claim a home child in their ancestry two or three or four generations back.

I know that some of you attended the talk given by Dr. Lawrence Patrick a few years ago. He's the Canadian-born scholar who now teaches at Trinity College in Dublin. His particular field of study is the Irish diaspora, but he has a keen interest in the home children as many of them were Irish. He has been here to look at our archives three times over the last ten years, and it's always a pleasure for us to receive him.

He has recently published a very interesting book dealing with the birth parents and families of home children. As you know, with some exceptions, home children were not orphans, but rather the children of people living in such poverty that they were unable to feed and clothe their offspring, and so sent them overseas, never to be seen again.

As Dr. Patrick points out, the players involved in the transportation of home children all acted from widely different motives. For the British government, this was an efficient and economical way of ridding the streets of urchins who were unsightly at best and actively criminal at worst. Churches and benevolent societies sent each child off with a small trunk of clothes, and the hope that however hard it might be in the new country, life would still be a little easier than in the old one. The Canadian government, like the governments of the other countries in the British Empire that took in tens of thousands of children every year, was glad to bring these children in; despite everything, they were British children, children largely from the Home Counties around London. British immigrants of course were considered, by far, the most desirable immigrants.

The excerpt that we're going to look at from Dr. Patrick's book paints the portrait of an Irish-born woman by the name of Iris O'Connell who lived in London in the second half of the nineteenth century:

Iris gripped the paddle with both hands, lifted it, and then thrust it with the full force of her one hundred and fifteen pounds into the sheets that rose ghostlike from the cauldron of boiling water. She forced the paddle as far as she could to the left, and then to the right, and then raised the paddle again to repeat the procedure.

The steam that rose from the cauldron was laced with lye, and so scalded Iris with a double intensity. Her hands, her forearms, and her face were permanently stained an angry red.

Iris was an inch and a half over five feet tall. To work the paddle, to be high enough above the cauldron to stir the boiling bed sheets, Iris climbed on a small stool that made her twenty inches taller.

Iris worked barefoot. She walked to the hospital in her shoes, but when she got down to the laundry room, she slipped them off her feet. There was no point in wearing out shoe leather if it wasn't necessary. Her bare soles were an advantage when she stood on the stool, her own skin less likely to slip than shoe leather. When she stepped off the stool and onto the flagstone floor, it was another matter. The floor was often wet in places, and always cold, unless scalding water had just been spilled on it. She felt all the irregularities of the stone surface when she walked, all the small nuggets, and shards, and grit of the coal that had to be brought from the bin to feed the stoves.

Iris was one of a dozen girls in the laundry, even if she was no longer a girl. She hadn't been a maid since she was fourteen, and she was thirty-four now. She was thirty-four and she was afraid that she was with child again. After the last one, she'd said never again, although she had said that before, had said it in fact after her first child had been born when she was seventeen. It seemed to her now that she had repeated those words after every birth. The last one was three years ago, and she'd told Liam, "No more." The child, a boy they had called Oliver, had died two months after he was born. The infant had taken a fever, turned red, and died, all in the space of a day.

But she had not been sorry, not fully sorry. Something inside her had felt something like relief. She had told no one about this feeling, had not even confessed it to the priest. In part, this was because it would have been difficult to put the emotions that simmered inside her into words. Though when it came to that, she made no effort, no real effort, to put into words, even for her own satisfaction, exactly what she felt about the loss of this last child. It was all better left unsaid. After all, what difference would words make?

Nor had Oliver been the first of her children to die. Twelve times Iris had fallen pregnant, and ten of those times she'd brought her child to term, but only seven of those children were still living. There'd been a girl, Kathleen, who had died at the age of five, and Thomas, who was eight when he had been kicked by a horse on Franklin Street, and died three days later. She had loved Kathleen, and she had deeply mourned Thomas, and words, even those spoken in church by the priest, had in no way helped.

And now, if she was again with child, as she greatly feared she was, Iris knew that words would be of no use. She sensed that words would only get in the way of what some instinct deep inside was struggling to dictate.

There was no clock in the laundry, no time piece to tell Iris how long the sheets had been boiling in the cauldron. They were, as Sister frequently reminded them, to boil for ten minutes, but it was only Sister who owned a timepiece. Sister came down to the laundry four or five times a day. She would stand a few steps inside the doorway, a spot from which she could see them all. She would plunge a hand deep into a black robe and pull out a silver pocket watch and flip it open. Sister would remain in the laundry long enough to give Iris, and the three other girls who boiled linen, their time. That is, she would note when a girl plunged the sheets into the cauldron, and she would call out, "Ten minutes!" to the girl ten minutes later, or perhaps, "Not yet! A full ten minutes," if someone had moved too soon to start removing the heavy material from the boiling water. Iris had developed a good sense of just how long "ten minutes" was.

Iris released her grip on the paddle and let it bob up and fall against the cauldron's edge. She climbed down from her small perch, and without hurry, crossed the stone floor to fetch an empty tub. Sometimes she exchanged a few words with Mary as she picked up the galvanized container, and sometimes she didn't. She carried it back to her post and placed it up against the cauldron, where it could easily receive the freshly boiled sheets. She retrieved a short paddle from its hook and climbed back up onto her stool.

Transferring the hot fabric from the boiling cauldron to the empty tub was when Iris had to be especially careful. She had seen it happen once, shortly after she had started work in the laundry. A cauldron of boiling water had tipped, had fallen from the stove top and splashed half its corrosive contents onto a girl, burning her badly from the waist down; she had suffered horribly for two days before she died. More frequently, girls burned their hands or arms, either from touching the stove, or the cauldron, or the water, or even the sheets.

Iris took hold of her paddle, thrust it into the water. When she was sure she felt a good clump of fabric at the end of her paddle, she pushed the heavy wad against the far bulge of the cauldron and lifted it towards the surface. By using the cauldron edge as a fulcrum, she could use the paddle as a lever to lift the sheet out of the water. She tried to lift it as high above the boiling liquid as possible, and then let the wet cotton balance there for a minute or so, hoping it might cool off to a more tolerable temperature. With her right hand on the paddle holding the fabric high, she used the shorter paddle in her left hand to support the wet sheet on the cauldron's lip. She pushed the longer paddle deeper into the water and lifted more of the fabric towards the surface. With five or six deft moves, Iris wrestled the first of the sheets into the waiting tub below. Each successive sheet was easier to remove than the previous one.

With the sheets still steaming, Iris picked up the galvanized tub, and carried it to Mary who would now have the task of running cold water over the material to start rinsing off the lye. Three times Mary would have to fill the tub and empty it, all the while swishing the sheets around as much as possible. As much as Iris suffered from the heat in the laundry, she knew that Mary suffered just as much from the cold.

Crossing the floor back to her stove, Iris cursed her life. Why was she here, sweating in a hellhole, pounding soiled bedsheets in tubs of boiling water? What for? To return to a hovel as cold and damp as the laundry was steaming hot? To return to a drunkard of a husband who ran hot and cold, when he wasn't running to the pub to drink his week's wages? To find herself again with child because she'd been unable to fend off a man who, drunk or sober, outweighed her by fifty pounds, and who'd left her with a black eye for her efforts? To have another child when she already had seven that she could hardly keep fed and clothed as it was?

No, thought Iris. She didn't want any of this. It was well and good for the priest to say that we all had a cross to bear, that a heavenly paradise awaited us on the other side of this vale of tears. But the priest was a rotund man who was well-fed and well shod and led a life well different from hers.

There were two hundred and thirty beds in the hospital, and sheets were changed every four days, except of course, for those patients who were in for less than four days, in which case they were changed when the patient was discharged, or when he died. There was always a large pile of sheets waiting to be washed. With each new wash, Iris had to add water to her cauldron along with a quarter cup of lye.

It always took a few minutes to bring the new water to a boil, and Iris fed her stove as necessary. When her fire ran low, she went to the coal bin to fill her pail. Almost always, she slid a few lumps of hard coal into the deep left-hand pocket of her dress. It was always the left, because the right was where she kept whatever food she might be able to bring to work; today she had a crust of bread and two carrots that she would eat when she and the others would be allotted a half hour for their noon meal. It wouldn't do to put coal in the wrong pocket, much as the coal was coveted. This was hard coal and it created little dust, but even that would spoil the taste of food. At home she burned soft coal, which was all she could afford; it gave a poor heat and burned too quickly. If she could bring home half a dozen lumps of hard coal, it was a halfpenny saved, and a little extra warmth.·

Iris shuffled and slogged through her day, and what formed in her mind did so of its own accord. It formed little by little, without conscious thought on her part, as if one element linked to another, which in turn led to another until it was a complete image that was at once terrible to contemplate, and yet so compelling, so sensible, so inevitable.

In her own way, Iris was an intelligent woman, resourceful, imaginative, and able to improvise. She had also learned patience. At the end of the day, as she walked home, she resolved to wait another week, just be sure. She was already sure, but she told herself, in this case, it was best to be doubly sure.

It was important today that she be happy with the children, that she make them laugh if she could. For them, this was to be an outing, a happy outing. For Iris this was a day to stay clearheaded and focused. She was aware that she was feeling just a little lightheaded, and she knew that it was because she hadn't eaten, but she wasn't going to eat. She wasn't going to take even a sip of water. She was going to concentrate on what she had to do, step by step. And she was going to be happy for them, and make them happy today, and, she fervently hoped, for the rest of their lives.

It wasn't yet a week since the thought had come to Iris, and in that time, she felt as if she had been living at a breakneck pace. Everything seemed to go so fast.

Yet somehow things had unfolded almost of their own accord. The very next day she had obtained the name of the woman on the Darlington Road, had walked there and found her almost immediately. The woman seemed nervous and hostile at first, and for a moment Iris was afraid she had made a mistake. But she had told the woman her situation nonetheless, and the mood had changed. The woman had opened her door to invite her in, and Iris had seen two rooms that were as spotless and tidy as any that Iris had ever seen. The woman asked her questions in a kindly voice and more and more Iris saw her as someone capable and trustworthy. "Sometimes," the woman said, "girls come here and want it done right away. It's best though, to fast the day before, and drink little water, none at all in the hours before you come here. It could be tomorrow if you want." Iris explained that she needed time, and the woman told her not to wait more than a week. They had set a date, the one day of the week that Iris had off.

Iris hoped a week would be enough because she faced two problems. She needed money, almost her full week's wages. More important, she had to think of something for the children, just in case, because Iris accepted as fact that she might not come back from Darlington Road.

On the long walk home, Iris's family situation, little by little, sorted itself out almost of its own accord and this, because, for some reason she couldn't explain, she began with Liam, her husband and father of her children. He came into her mind, and almost immediately she wanted to cast him out. Liam, and the thought startled her when it came, would be the one good thing about not coming back from Darlington Road. She wanted no more of him, no more of his drunken rages, no more of his slovenly ways. She couldn't understand what had ever led her to be with him. She couldn't remember him in any way other than the way he was now, although she knew he must have been different, as she herself was different now to what she had been. He was like a stranger to her, she thought, a stranger who lived in her house, who was the source of her trouble. She would be glad, she said aloud to no one as she hurried towards her home, if she never saw him again.

With a conscious effort, she turned her thoughts to Patrick who was seventeen now, and who would soon be finding a home of his own. He had always been a little slow moving and she had worried about him, perhaps more than any of her other children, but she took some pride in him now. He was in his third year of apprenticeship to Mr. Williams, the tailor in Marsh Lane and next year he would start earning full wages, if not from Mr. Williams, from some other shop, because there was always work for tailors. He was almost a grown man, Patrick, and she realized that he now had hardly any need for her at all.

Nor did Fianna any longer have much need of her. She was almost fifteen, and, for two years now she had been working at the hose factory, and bringing home most of her wages. Lately, Iris had noticed, Fianna had started keeping more and more of those wages for herself, and not putting very much into the money jar that was kept on the kitchen shelf. Fianna had explained that she had to buy a new smock for work, and then that she needed new shoes, and these expenditures necessarily reduced her contribution to the household. Then last week, Fianna again had put only a small part of her wages into the money jar but had given no explanation as to where the rest of her money had gone, or what she had done with it. There had been other changes in Fianna, and although Iris had so far said nothing, had not asked any questions, she sensed that her daughter had met a boy, as she herself had done at much the same age. Fianna, like Patrick, no longer had any real need of her.

The same was almost true for Nial and Sean, Iris thought. They weren't much younger than Fianna, thirteen and twelve, and both strong boys, unlike their older brother. Both were working now, Nial as an apprentice for Peterson, the carter and Sean as an errand boy for the costermonger. They weren't yet making full salaries, but they were both good about putting their weekly wages into the money jar, at least so far. Nial was not a concern, but Iris had worries about Sean, who, she feared, had something too much of Liam about him. They might miss their mother, Iris thought, but they too had reached a point at which they could manage without her.

This left the three youngest ones, and all three, Iris knew, would still need a mother, or at least someone to care for them. Liam would not. Liam would be gone the next day, as soon as he saw there was no one there to put his supper on the table. He would leave without a thought for the children.

Iris arrived home hours late. There had been an accident at the laundry, she told Liam, and she stayed longer because they needed the help. He moved to slap her, but she saw a moment of doubt in his eye, and she didn't raise her arms in defense. She looked at him with her head straight. He turned away from her, growling that she had better get paid for her extra hours.

Fianna had eventually boiled potatoes for her father and siblings, but what food she had prepared had all been eaten. There was oatmeal, and not much else, on the kitchen shelf. Iris waited till she heard Liam's soft snoring before going to bed.

For two days Iris thought about the three youngest, Colleen who was nine, and Brendan and Colm, who were seven and almost six. The orphanage, she knew, would take them after she was gone. In her mind, it was clear that Liam would abandon the children. After he left, she imagined, Fianna would be the one to go to the parish priest, and the parish priest would haul the three youngest ones to the orphanage, and perhaps Nial and Sean as well, although they were working, and could almost fend for themselves. But she couldn't bring them to the orphanage if she and the children's father were both still alive. There was something else about the orphanage that made her hesitate although she was unable to put into words what it was.

It was a snippet of conversation that she overheard on the street that solved the problem of the youngest ones. What Iris overheard was a woman, holding a child no older than her Colleen by the hand, asking for directions to the Quaker Home.

Iris knew of the Quakers, although she mistrusted much of what she had heard about them. She had never met a Quaker herself, at least not as far as she knew, so she had no first-hand knowledge on which she might rely. She had always been told that, like all Protestants, Quakers were doomed to the fires of hell, and that they were somehow even worse than other Protestants. Yet, she had also heard, on more than one occasion, that they were God-fearing people who strove to love others as they loved God. She had also heard that they were committed to good works. Somehow, she tended to believe they were good people.

What she learned later that day she believed as well.

"Have you heard of the Quaker Home?" she asked Mary as casually as she could, adding, "I heard someone on the street today asking where it is."

"Down by Trotters Lane," Mary told her, "but why would you want to know something like that?"

"No reason, I just heard someone ask about it."

"It's like an orphanage, you know, but not like St. Joseph's," Mary rushed on. "They look after them well, is what they say, and they find homes for them all across the Empire. They send them to Australia, to Canada. Better off there, if you ask me. For them that's born with a silver spoon in their mouth it's all plum pudding. They say there's opportunities in the colonies, even for the likes of us."

On Saturday, the day she received her week's wages, Iris brought her winter stockings to work. They were rolled up and shoved into the pocket where she normally carried whatever food she might bring with her to the laundry. They were bulky enough that Iris knew there was no danger they would slip through the small hole in the pocket. The hole Iris had made was very small, only big enough to slide two fingers through.

When she received her wages, she turned back towards the laundry and stepped into the privy where she pulled out her winter stockings. The money she normally put into her pocket, she carefully slipped into her stockings. Almost all of the money went into the left stocking. This was the money she would need for herself, for the woman on the Darlington Road. What was left went into her right stocking and was for her last day with the young ones.

As she expected, Liam was furious. Yet, as she watched his eyes, she saw that her story had convinced him. The hole, when she drew the pocket from her dress, was impossible to deny. Without those wages, he yelled, how were they to pay for the coal, and the rent? She knew that his fury stemmed from knowing that he wouldn't have money to spend in the pub.

He slapped her, which she expected as inevitable, but he only hit her once, in part because her story had convinced him, but also because she had yelled back at him, cursed him, and as much from surprise at her response as from anything else, he was startled and stopped.

And so today she was waking the three young ones early. Very quietly she would slip out of the house with the three of them. There was enough money for the four of them to take a tram almost to Trotter's Lane. It was the beginning of an adventure, she would tell them, an adventure that would perhaps take them half-way around the world, and wouldn't that be exciting!

She would be happy with them, and leave them at the Quaker House, and then take the long walk to Darlington Road.

Chapter 26

We want to thank Dr. Lawrence Patrick for that back-story on the home children.

You will have noticed that in Dr. Patrick's narrative the young girl about to be put into the hands of the Quakers to later be sent oversees is named Colleen, the same name as the home child serving as a maid in the Spicker household. We would like to think that it is the same person although we have no way of verifying that, and in truth, it is highly unlikely.

In Dr. Patrick's narrative, Iris O'Connell survived her back-street abortion and lived to the relatively ripe old age of seventy-six. At the time, women in England had a life expectancy of forty-nine; as a working-class woman, Iris would not have been expected to live long beyond that. I won't tell you her entire story (Dr. Patrick did that in his book, a very good read I should add, and we have a few copies for sale at the museum) but even if I don't tell you her entire life story, I will tell you that she died, not in London, but in her native Ireland, where she lies buried in Rockgrove, a small village just outside of Cork.

Whether she was Colleen O'Connell, daughter of Iris O'Connell who died in Rockgrove, or another Colleen entirely, the Colleen who worked for the Spickers nevertheless was integral to the death of Ralph Andosca. She did not fire the gun that killed him. She didn't even know him. But had there been no Colleen, there would not have been a murder.

We know that because of this next passage from our diarist, which is also one of the last.

Day ten

I am glad to say that I have solved the mystery of the voices in the night! But let me start with the morning.

It did not bode well. CS continues to hound me to finish my needlepoint. I may have to adopt Penelope's tactic and silently slip downstairs every night to undo my day's work. My frame is advancing at a snail's pace but, however slowly I go, it grows nearer completion every day. This morning, promptly at nine o'clock CS called me down to the parlour to persist with our frames. She sat nearby and assiduously pushed her needle through her canvas and back again at a furious pace. She might have been racing a steam engine, the rate at which she was going. She is working on quite a large piece that is mounted on a stand and eventually will result in one more wall hanging for a house which is already full of them. My piece is thankfully small, and I work with the frame in my lap. At CS's insistence, when completed (which it will never be) the piece I am working on should result in the word 'Mother' stitched in red on a cream background and it is supposed to be a gift for Mater. This idea, it goes without saying, came from CS.

As I pushed my needle back and forth, I kept having visions of putting my needle through CS's eyes, or better yet sewing her mouth shut to cease her continuous prattle. CS has an opinion on everything and the more foolish her opinions the more enthusiastically and vociferously she expounds upon them. When she is not promoting nonsense, she is salaciously smearing all and sundry. She is the most frightful gossip and has something disagreeable to say about anyone and everyone.

Eventually I had had enough and took drastic action. I intentionally stabbed the needle into the fleshy pad of my fingertip. I

185

squeezed my finger hard to get as many drops of blood as possible to drip over my needlepoint.

CS literally leaped to my rescue, reacting as if I'd severed my arm or as if I had haemophilia like the late Queen. Top-heavy as she is, it was a wonder poor CS didn't topple and crash to the floor. If the sight of my blood disturbed her, it was with mixed emotions for the next moment she wasn't sure if she should be more worried about my injury (I had no intention of assuring her that it was insignificant, and especially not that it had been self-inflicted) or about the blood that was staining my needlepoint (this too was intentional; wanting to I could have cupped my hand so as to let no blood drip anywhere at all other than into my palm).

It was easy, shortly after, to go out for a walk. I believe that I am finally beginning to exasperate CS and she was noticeably glad to have me leave the house. As I had hoped, CS instructed Colleen to leave what she was doing and accompany me. Since my second day when I had to argue with CS for half an hour to be permitted to take a stroll (exercise, I argued forcefully, was important to the health of a growing adolescent), she has insisted that I not walk anywhere on my own, and has had Colleen accompany me. "You need not walk with her, Dear, she can trail a step or two behind you, but you simply can't walk on the street alone."

I've no doubt that CS would be mortified to know that Colleen does not walk two steps behind me but rather that we walk together, and furthermore that we quite enjoy our conversations which have been far ranging when they have not been about CS herself.

I was especially anxious to speak to Colleen today and as soon as we were out of sight of CS, (who always sees us off by standing at the front window with the sheer curtains pulled aside just enough to bang her long nose on the window pane) I asked her about the voices that I heard last night.

What happened is that I read quite late into the evening, and before retiring to bed I took my lamp, slipped into my shoes, and walked back to the privy. (Much as the privy is rather loathsome, it is preferable to using a chamber pot, which then stays pushed under the bed for the entire night! To date, I have refrained from using it, and it goes without saying that I shan't ever use it.)

It was late, after midnight, and I imagined that everyone was asleep. Yet, as I stepped out of the back door, I thought I heard voices and soft laughter. I stopped, and turned towards the clothesline stoop, which is where the voices seemed to have come from, and held the lamp up as high as I could but of course the voices, wherever they may have been coming from, had fallen silent. I looked around but all there was to see, really, were shadows, cast by the few small trees (supposedly plum and apple although there is no fruit on any of them) and by the carriage house. I stood still for a few minutes and listened but all was silent.

On the way back to the house, I walked quite slowly and stopped a couple of times, holding the lamp up high and looking around me, but there was nothing or no one to be seen.

I told all this to Colleen, and I was surprised by her silence which lasted until she asked, "But, you didn't see anyone?"

It took a long time—we walked as far as the new dam built across the river by the paper company—but I finally found out that what I heard last night was indeed someone, in fact two someones: Colleen and a young man who has been coming to visit her. It was they who were sitting on the clothesline stoop when my appearance startled them. They crouched as low as they could, and they remained perfectly still. They were far enough away that they were nothing more than shadows in the faint light cast by my oil lamp. The moment I closed the privy door, they slipped silently around the side of the house and away.

This is a young man that Colleen met earlier this summer. Four times now, he has come to meet her at night. They find a spot—like the stoop—where they can sit and talk.

"There's no other time for us to meet, is there? I'm at Mrs. Spicker's beck and call all day long. Even on my half day off, I'm accountable to her, and have to tell her where I'm going, and what I'm doing, and who will be there. And unless it's a church social, she disapproves of me going anywhere.

"So we meet when we can, and that's at night. Sometimes I do see him for a few minutes in the afternoon, but that only happens three times a week, and it's never for very long."

Colleen didn't want to tell me his name. "I'm superstitious," she said. "It's too soon. I'm afraid that if I tell anyone his name, that he'll disappear."

She did tell me that it is not the young man of whom CS has been complaining. That young man is Samuel Brightwood, he of the horticulturally inclined horse. I know from CS that Samuel Brightwood is a home boy, a home child like Colleen (not that CS would admit as much about Colleen). He works on the farm of Mr. James Traynor, an old bachelor who lives a mile or so down the River Road. I have seen Samuel at the house often enough to agree that CS (for a change) is not incorrect that he comes by on rather flimsy excuses and stays much longer than he should. I thought that after the episode with the flowers he might be reluctant to show his face again, but no, he was back at the house two days later. He came to the kitchen door—as he always does—and made a point—again as he always does—of addressing CS even though it's Colleen he wants to talk to. He apologized profusely for the loss of CS's flowers and explained that he had brought a brace of rabbits that he had just shot by way of atonement. He held out the two hares dangling by their hind legs with one arm and cradled his long gun casually in the other. He had just shot the poor animals and knew that Mrs. Spicker liked rabbit stew, and again he wanted to say how sorry he was about the flowers. CS told him to give the animals to Colleen and to be on his way.

"Yes, Ma'am," he said but then turned to Colleen to tell her how to go about preparing a rabbit stew, as if it were something that she didn't already know.

"Out!" CS screamed at him.

As calmly as if he hadn't heard, Brightwood said, "Goodbye, Ma'am. I hope you enjoy the stew," put his battered old hat on his head and glided out the door.

Colleen knows that Samuel, who is twenty-three and engaged year-round by Mr. Traynor, is sweet on her, but she cares nothing at all for him. "I imagine that when I turn eighteen, and am free, he is going to propose," she said. "He was a home boy and he assumes that just because I was a home child as well that I should be glad to have him. He earns a fair wage, and he even has a small cabin on Mr. Traynor's property that Mr. Traynor told him to consider as his own. But I don't care for Samuel, and I never have. At one time, it didn't bother me that he took forever to leave eggs, or butter, or apples, or whatever. It was more pleasant talking with him in the kitchen than having Mrs. S nagging me for something. But I have never cared for Samuel and I think he must be quite dense if he is not aware of that."

Whom she does care for is the boy—or perhaps I should say young man, for he is Colleen's age—she was with last night,

He's an American, from New York State and he's working on the construction of a rail line that's supposed to come right here, to Greenlay, although he's not a labourer but a cook. She met him quite by accident when she went to the spring to fetch drinking water. He had stopped to water his team of horses. Since then, they manage to meet at the spring almost every second day, and lately, he sometimes comes to see her at night, as he did last night.

Colleen sleeps in a small porch attached to the summer kitchen. As all the bedrooms are on the second floor, she can quite easily slip out the kitchen door without anyone being any the wiser.

Her young man will be working until the rail line is finished, or until the snow comes which might be as early as the end of October, or as late as December, and then she will go off with him.

She will have her freedom before then, as she turns eighteen in September. She expects that the Spickers will want her to stay on, even if they will have to start paying her a salary, but if they don't, she is confident of finding temporary work somewhere nearby.

She promised me to secrecy on all of this, and I gave it without hesitation. Why ever would I say anything at all to CS? No, I am ever so excited for Colleen, and ever so happy for her. If not for her, I think I would have gone completely mad in this house.

Chapter 27

There are only a few more entries in the diary, but I wanted to stop for a second to tell you that the passage we just looked at is the one that allows us to examine the murder of young Ralph Andosca from another angle. Had he seen the murder of young Ralph Andosca from this angle, High Constable Roderick Moe would certainly have had a suspect; a suspect with a murder weapon and, more importantly, with a motive.

I'm being a little unfair, I realize. You have only just seen this last passage while I went back to it a couple of times, and that over the course of several days, so that I had a lot more time than you to sift through the details and allow the significant ones to make themselves seen.

I do though want you to look at the last entries because they're quite short and I think you'll get a chuckle out of some of them, because I know I did.

My last night!

The telegram arrived just as we were about to sit down to supper, as it is called in the Spicker household. I knew before it was handed to me what it would say. My heart skipped a beat, but I forced myself to show not a shred of emotion. I took my time opening it and read it three times over before I lifted my head and with the dullest voice I could muster said only, "I will have to catch the train at 9:30 tomorrow morning. Could someone pass the butter, please?"

CS did not pass the butter, but she did gasp audibly, and when she recovered her breath, she grew overly excited with an endless list of needless anxieties. Will I have time to pack? Wouldn't I want CS to lend her invaluable help with my packing? Will I be sure not to forget anything? Will I not forget to bring my needlepoint? There is so little left to do, might I not want to finish it on the train going home? Wasn't it wonderful how the bloodstains had come out? Will I remember to tell Mater what a wonderful time we all had, and tell her that her cousins would adore it if she too could come for a visit? (Especially if it were next year after the house will finally have indoor plumbing!)

I had to fight CS all the way up the stairs to my room; that's how determined she was that I needed her help to pack.

What a surprise I had waiting for me! I pulled my two suitcases from under the bed where they've been keeping the chamber pot company and when I opened them, to my astonishment, in one of them were a few odds and ends that I had never unpacked, and there, at the bottom of the suitcase was a letter that I was to have given to Cousin John. His name was on the envelope but only that, not his full address, and the envelope felt unnaturally thick. The flap had not been sealed shut but only tucked into the back.

I couldn't resist the temptation and so I carefully lifted the flap and drew out the contents. The letter to Cousin John was very short (and not very flattering towards me) but the surprise was that along with the letter (inside it, as the sheet was folded in three) were two hundred dollars for my upkeep. For that kind of money, I could have stayed at one of the better hotels! I put the letter and money back in the envelope, placed it on my desk, and set about packing my things.

One suitcase is all packed and clasped shut; the other is on the floor at the foot of my bed, ready to receive my nightdress and toiletries, the book I'm still reading, and my diary. Those I will put in tomorrow at the last minute just before I leave.

I've decided that Cousin John will get Mater's letter tomorrow, and I will leave him one hundred dollars for my upkeep—even that is, in my opinion, overly generous. They can't have spent a tenth of that to feed me over the last ten days; oatmeal for breakfast and boiled potatoes and ham for supper—hardly meals fit for a king, or even a princess.

The other hundred dollars I am going to leave to Colleen. I had already planned to leave her a small gratuity from the allowance that I have hardly touched. I shall keep just a few dollars for my trip home but the rest of my allowance I will leave to Colleen and with the hundred dollars from the envelope it will make a nice early birthday present for her.

I have come to admire Colleen very much, and I do wish her well with her beau.

I think I shall read a little more of Penelope Farthing and then turn my lamp out early this evening.

Tomorrow night I shall be sleeping again in my own bed!

8:00 a.m.

I woke up to a bright, sunny day as if the gods agree with me that today is a radiantly joyous one.

The first thing at breakfast, I gave Cousin John Mater's letter and loot and explained to him how I had been negligent in noticing it when I unpacked.

He laughed (a little nervously I thought) as he surreptitiously slipped the envelope into the inside breast pocket of his jacket. "I don't have time to read it now," he said, "but tell your mother I'll write back as soon as I can."

I wonder if I shall miss CS and her constant prattle?

You will tell your mother what a joy it was to have you here! You will tell her we would be so glad to have you come and visit again! You got along so well with Dixon-Albert! You will tell her how much you enjoyed yourself here! You will keep in touch with Dixon-Albert, I'm sure! We were so glad to have you!

Red-faced Cousin John and Dixon-Albert of the pimply forehead both left for work as usual, Cousin John apologizing for not being able to accompany us to catch the train, but assuring us that one of his men will be back with the buggy to drive me to the station.

In a few minutes I'll be leaving in the company of the billowing sails of CS...

I've just written a short note to Colleen which I will leave here for her to find...

Chapter 28

There, the screen is off. Thank you, Shaun.

That was how the diary entries came to an end. The remaining half-dozen pages are blank.

Somehow, our diarist left her diary behind when she quit the house to catch her train; otherwise how could it have ended up in Belinda Clark's possession? It's easy to imagine that it was Colleen who found the diary, along with the note and the money that were intended for her, when she went upstairs to the young diarist's room to change the sheets and sweep and clean the room. Did she think of giving the diary to Mrs. Spicker? Did she possibly, probably, open it and read parts of it? If so, she would certainly have kept the diary from her employer. Perhaps she would have kept it with the intention of mailing it herself to the young diarist, if she could manage to find her address.

But, even with the best of intentions, plans go awry. Colleen must have kept the diary, probably hidden in some secret spot where it was found years later, perhaps after her death, by an heir who saw an attractive cover, a nice book to pass on to Belinda, or perhaps her spinster aunt, Florence Underwood, and from there came to our archives. Was it ever read by Florence Underwood, or Belinda Clark, or anyone else? We don't know.

We are grateful though that the diary survived because it sheds a new light on the murder of Ralph Andosca. High

Constable Moe wondered if the murder of the twelve-year-old was an act of revenge vicariously carried out against the victim's father. Moe was actually close to the mark. The murder was revenge, but revenge of a different kind directed against a different Andosca. The murder was a crime of passion. It was the act of a jealous suitor who with one quick squeeze of a trigger sought to permanently eliminate his rival. When Samuel Brightwood squeezed the trigger, it was seventeen-year-old Tyler Andosca and not twelve-year-old Ralph whom he intended to target.

How could such a thing come about? It's clear from the diary that Samuel Brightwood had known Colleen for quite some time, and for some time had harboured hopes that she might be as interested in him as he was in her. There's no doubt that he had been subtly (or perhaps not so subtly) wooing her for some time.

And then he discovered that she was interested in another. Would he have seen Colleen talking to Tyler at the spring? Would he have heard from Mrs. Heriot that the Spicker's maid seemed very friendly with the young Italian who came to town every other day? In a small town, as we all know, news spreads quickly. Was there a confrontation of some kind between the two suitors? Was Tyler Andosca's bruised cheekbone not the result of an accident in the stable but rather of a fight with Samuel Brightwood? Did Brightwood, in a fit of rage, decide that if fists could not dissuade his rival, then a firearm certainly would?

Was this a plan that Brightwood hatched over a day or two, or was it a spontaneous, impulsive decision to kill his rival? Samuel Brightwood had access to a gun. He also had relatively easy access to the Orford Mountain Railway's right of way, for it ran only a short distance behind the Traynor farm where Brightwood worked. He needed only a brief window of time to leave his chores, make his way through a quarter mile of bush and go in pursuit of his victim.

Was he doggedly making his way towards the construction camp when he first spotted the wagon and the trailing horseman at a distance? From a distance, did he see a twelve-year-old boy? Almost certainly not. Ralph Andosca was big for his age, and he bore a close resemblance to his older brother. From a distance one could pass for the other. It's easy to imagine that Samuel Brightwood thought that it was Tyler Andosca that he saw trailing behind Richard Todd.

Seeing them further up the roadbed, did he duck for the nearest cover, the large mound of debris near the side of the well-beaten subgrade that provided him with a suitable, but not ideal, hiding place? If he wanted to remain hidden from them, he had to remain flattened against the mound. He had to rely on his ears to measure their approach, to know when they were opposite the mound, and when they had passed it.

With a different weapon, Brightwood might have had more time to measure up his victim, but he only had a small shotgun designed for small game. To kill a man, Brightwood knew that he would have to be close to his victim.

He waited, no doubt nervously, listening to the approach of squeaky wagon wheels, straining to hear the hoof beats of the horseman following behind. He had to wait for both to pass him, yet he could not wait too long. When he moved, he had to move quickly. A half-dozen strides to the roadbed, a second to raise the gun, aim, and squeeze the trigger. Instantly to turn, dash behind the mound, and disappear into the woods.

High Constable Moe, had he known about Brightwood, would have found him easily, would have found his gun and sent it to Montreal for testing, and known within a few days if it was indeed the murder weapon.

Our young diarist left Greenlay on the same day that Ralph Andosca was murdered. Did she hear of the murder? Possibly, but not necessarily. And Colleen, was she aware of Brightwood's temper, of his jealous rage? Did she suspect him as a murderer? Perhaps not, for it wasn't Tyler who had been killed. And, in her situation, even if she conceived of the killing as a case of mistaken identity, to whom would she have gone with her story, a story of which she was a part that she would have wanted to keep secret?

Would anyone else have been aware that Colleen had two suitors? That one sought revenge on the other?

As I mentioned before, history has a way of leaving questions in its wake even when occasional answers are found.

I see Margaret at the back, pointing at her wristwatch. I may have taken more than the half hour that I was supposed to talk, so I will end it there, ladies and gentlemen.

The answer to the question, why—why was a twelve-year-old boy shot dead in Melbourne Township on the afternoon of August 16, 1905—is that it was a tragic mistake involving a man acting in an uncontrolled fit of jealousy and a victim who bore a close resemblance to his older brother, the intended victim.

Thank you very much.

I don't know if we have time for questions. Margaret? Margaret says just one.

No?

No one?

Yes.

Ah! Now that's an interesting question, and the answer is yes, the Farnham Murder was "solved," in a manner of speaking, although no one ever did jail time, or was ever brought to justice in any way.

Chapter 29

The other boy murder of 1905, the murder in Farnham of four-teen-year-old Wilfrid Audette, was a far more sensational—and disturbing—case.

Arrests were made; a week or so after the murder, three hobos—three men of no fixed address is the way the *Record* would describe them today, but hobos was the word used by the *Sherbrooke Daily Record* back then—three men riding a freight car were picked up by the police in Ottawa on suspicion of murder. They were questioned but a few days later they were released without any charges being laid. No other arrests were ever made in the case.

Given the prominence of the family name, Wilfrid Audette's death was much harder on the people of Farnham than Ralph Andosca's death was on the people of Melbourne Township. It was an event that remained in the public consciousness for two generations or more. If anything, the Farnham Murder, because of its brutality, was even more mystifying than the murder on the Orford Mountain Railway. Why would anyone want to pound a boy to death with a rock?

What I'm going to recount comes from a short but interest-ing book that was published at the very end of the last century. It's titled *Ten Percent of What You Hear* and it was written by Dimitry Karlovitch, who was Russian-born but came to Canada as a child and lived most of his life in the Farnham area where, among other things, he was a stringer for the *Sherbrooke Daily Record*. For the better part of five decades he submitted articles to the *Record* on an infrequent and irregular basis as a freelance reporter. Shortly before he died, he published a book, an autobiographical account of his peregrinations through the Eastern Townships in search of stories.

Karlovitch did some reporting for the *Record* (a paper that in the span of his career changed names from the *Sherbrooke Daily Record* to the *Sherbrooke Record* to the *Record*) but most of his stories were what would be called soft news, and typically the stories would be quite interesting without being actual news. They were often longer, feature pieces that would have more naturally have fit in a magazine rather than a newspaper.

The title of his book is a reference to advice he was given when he first stepped into the newsroom of the *Sherbrooke Daily Record*. The person who took him under his wing his first day was the assistant editor, an archetypically crusty old newsman by the name of Len Tobbins, who told him, "If you're going to be any good as a newspaperman, you want to remember that you write one tenth of what you hear, and even less of what you see." It's possible that Karlovitch followed that advice.

In the preface to his book, he refers to its contents as his untold stories.

One of these stories is a warm and sympathetic portrait of an octogenarian reflecting back on his Olympic glory and the years that followed. Gale Grant had represented Canada in two rowing events at the London Olympics in 1908: as a member of the men's eights, and as a silver medalist in the coxless fours. The following year, Grant graduated from McGill but stayed on to do postgraduate work. In 1914, immediately after the war broke out, he enlisted in the army. As befitting his class (the Grants were a well-to-do family in the Farnham area) and his education (at this point he had two university degrees, rare at the time), he was given a captain's commission and he rose to the rank of major. He survived the war, having spent much of it in England, and returned home a hero. Instead of returning to McGill to complete his doctoral studies, he embarked on a career in finance, first with the Eastern Townships Bank, and then with the Bank of Montreal. Gale Grant retired to North Hatley where Karlovitch interviewed him in 1968.

Grant passed away just three weeks after the interview.

In that interview Gale Grant talked about his Olympic glory and his financial success, but he also talked about something else, something that happened in the summer of 1905, and was more than anything else, a deathbed confession.

In 1904 Gale Grant started his first year at McGill where he made very good friends with a second-year student. The following summer, in August of 1905, his friend came to visit him on the weekend of the 12th. The friend was going to be leaving on the first train in the morning, and the two had gone out for a late evening walk on Saturday night even though it had been raining or drizzling off and on for most of the day. The sky remained dry for them and the walk had become quite long and led them to the back of the lumberyard, close to the CPR tracks.

The boy had appeared so suddenly that they were caught almost unawares. All at once, he was there with his bright light.

It was no good trying to slip away or trying to hide.

The boy recognized Grant, even before he recognized the boy—a neighbourhood boy he didn't like: a braggart, a bully, a noisy, boisterous boy. For a moment, the boy said nothing, but then he smirked, and laughed and began to make vulgar and obscene comments.

Grant warned him. He warned him twice.

If they didn't catch him, he would tell everyone. He was a fairly big boy, and strong, but they were bigger, and stronger, and faster.

And they caught him.

The boy had turned and started running, swinging that big lantern. Then he had stumbled and dropped his lantern. His friend had picked up the rock that had caused the boy to trip, and he had thrown it, and caught the boy in the back with enough force that the boy fell, and then they were on him. It wasn't what they wanted.

It shouldn't have happened.

His friend took the morning train and Grant never saw him again.

Dimitri Karlovitch points out that in 1905, a homosexual act was a crime, one for which Oscar Wilde had been imprisoned only ten years earlier.

Gale Grant lived long enough to hear Pierre Elliot Trudeau say that the government had no business in the bedrooms of the nation.

At another time, the grisly murder would never have occurred.

I see Margaret waving at me so I really must finish my talk on that note.

Thank you all very much for having been such a patient audience.

Acknowledgements

Several people contributed significantly to this book.

First and foremost, I want to thank Robin Philpot for once again taking a chance on my literary endeavours. A number of people read early drafts of this text and their comments and suggestions have made the text cleaner and richer, the details more precise and more accurate. To Jim Napier, Jacques Beaubien, Esther Healy, David Fonda, and Norma Husk, a big thank you. Thanks as well to Blossom Thom, Gaby Beland, and Beatrice Multhaupt. And a special thanks to Francine and Karine, my most discerning readers.

NOTABLE FICTION FROM BARAKA BOOKS

A Stab at Life
A Mystery Novel by Richard King

Fog
Rana Bose

Yasmeen Haddad Loves Joanassi Maqaittik
Carolyn Marie Souaid

Things Worth Burying
Matt Mayr

Exile Blues
Douglas Gary Freeman

NONFICTION

The PS Royal William of Quebec
The First True Transatlantic Steamer
Eileen Reid Marcil

Stolen Motherhood
Surrogacy and Made-to-Order Children
Maria De Koninck (translated by Arielle Aaronson)

Still Crying for Help
The Failure of Our Mental Healthcare Services
Sadia Messaili (translated by Aleshia Jensen)

Free of 'Incurable' Cancer, Living in Overtime
Susan Paton

Through the Mill
Girls and Women in the Quebec Cotton Textile Industry 1881-1951
Gail Cuthbert Brandt

Printed by Imprimerie Gauvin
Gatineau, Québec